THE FIRES OF ARCADIA

THE FIRES
OF ARCADIA

G. B. HARRISON

HARCOURT, BRACE & WORLD, INC.

NEW YORK

Sir Tristram: These, then, be the names which gentlemen use for creatures in their multitudes: a herd of deer, a gaggle of geese (but if they be on the wing, then are they a skein), a skulk of foxes, a school of herring, a pride of lions.

Philomathes: But, master, what of a party of satyrs?

Sir Tristram: You shall call them an HEAT OF SATYRS, for they be very hot, lustful beasts, soon kindled but hardly quenched.

—*Sir Tristram's Observations*
on the Art of Venery

THE FIRES OF ARCADIA

I

IN MY SEVENTEENTH YEAR AT ARCADIA COLLEGE
I was awarded a Gluckstein Fellowship for Study
in Europe. I planned to fly to London at the end
of January and there to put in a few months un-
interrupted research at the Public Record Office and the British Museum. In the spring my
wife would join me with the two children.

3

About eight o'clock in the evening I boarded my plane at Boston and was given a window seat. The plane was not much more than half filled and I hoped that with luck I would have the row to myself, but shortly before take-off, I was wedged in by a large man of about forty-five years who at first glance was a good specimen of the Executive Type. He had the air of one who issues commands and makes decisions. His face seemed familiar yet I could not place him.

He introduced himself. "Joe Fletcher, Monadnock Fire and Life Insurance of Boston."

I retorted with "Peter Lowe, Arcadia College, New Hampshire."

"Professor?"

"Yes," said I, "of history."

He looked at me closely.

"I guess we've met before."

Then I remembered. We had met, two days after the great fire. He was then an inspector, or whatever they called it, of fire claims, a very inquisitive suspicious inspector. I disliked him at sight, quite unjustly, for he was only doing his duty, and in a most competent way. Now he was vice-president in some other company, and in charge of personnel. It would be foolish to resent him, but I would not willingly have chosen Joe Fletcher as my companion for that flight. Trans-

4

atlantic flights take a long time and there is no escape from one's seat-mate.

"You have a good memory," I replied.

"You need it in my job."

Soon we took off and the plane rose over the ocean. Drinks were served, and ultimately dinner. We ate our meal in silence, but my companion— or jailer—was obviously eager to talk. I was not, at least not about the occasion of our first meeting. At the time it had been difficult enough fending off the curiosity of colleagues who were ignorant of the facts. This man already knew too much. But there was no escape. As soon as the trays were removed he began.

"That fire at Arcadia was a classic."

"I suppose it was," I agreed guardedly. "It cost the College three million dollars. But I expect that you've seen bigger fires."

"Heaps," he replied. "But that fire was the only case I've met where no claim was made on the insurance company. Fishy, wasn't it?"

He looked at me sideways as if I was responsible.

"There were, I understand, good reasons," said I, but in a tone which would have discouraged further comment from anyone with nice feelings. Joe Fletcher was not that kind of person. He neither took nor even perceived hints. Hardly the sensitive type, I thought.

5

"I guess there must have been," he commented, and in a most unpleasant tone. "I was a younger man then and I certainly hoped there would be a claim."

"But why? It saved your company three million dollars."

"May be; but it lost me the case of my life."

"How so?"

"If you had claimed, we would have disputed it and demanded a full inquiry. It was as clear a case of arson as I have ever seen."

I don't know in medical terms just what does happen to one's insides when one gets a bad shock; but at his words I felt as if there had been an earthquake in my stomach. I am, I suppose, rather a nervous person, and although I have been privately assured that the statute of limitations and other merciful enactments, not to mention lack of evidence, have long since freed me from all possible or at least likely legal consequences, nevertheless from time to time I still dream of policemen and electric chairs. However, Mr. Fletcher knew nothing of this or of my direct connection with the famous Arcadia fire. If asked I would pretend bland ignorance of the details.

"Arson?" said I, in a surprised tone. "How could anyone tell how that fire started? There wasn't much left of the old place next morning."

"I said arson," he insisted. "To an expert it was

as clear as gin. That fire was started in at least three places, probably more. Fires don't break out simultaneously in several places unless someone lights them."

"All the same I should be interested to know why you are so confident that it was arson."

"I'll tell you. That old building was built like a German castle, the sort of thing you see on picture postcards. Central building rectangular, with a high narrow roof, and turrets at each corner. Am I right?"

"Yes," I agreed; "it was like that."

"Well, the fire destroyed the main building pretty completely. A thorough job. But an arsonist, especially an amateur, always tries too hard. The turrets were intact, but in two of them minor fires had been started, and they had gone out. What do you say to that?"

I could say nothing to that. So I was silent. But Joe Fletcher was warming up.

"There was another thing. That guy whose body was found. The story that he went into the building to rescue his papers was plain phony."

How on earth, thought I, could he prove it? I ventured a protest.

"Why do you say that? I understood that only a few burnt bones were left."

"In a fire of that kind," he explained patiently, "a body sometimes is just burnt up till there's

7

hardly anything left, but the skull is usually intact, more or less. It takes an awful lot to destroy a human skull. And the guy who owned that skull died from a crack on the head. You see that sort of crack in the old skulls dug up where there has been a battle with Indians."

"Oh," said I. This man knew too much. All the same I added guilelessly, "If that is so, I wonder who could have done it."

He glowered at me suspiciously.

"I guess some people knew and kept it quiet. You were lucky that there wasn't a police inquiry."

We were indeed, I said to myself. He went on, "I showed that skull to the Police Chief at Linton. It was his job to set things going. He just wasn't interested. That was fishy too."

He snorted indignantly.

"But it wasn't the business of my company to prosecute or take action if no claim was made. I made my report and that just ended the case for me. Disappointing all the same. A queer business which I never could fathom."

He looked at me, hoping perhaps that I would be more communicative. I merely observed that it was all very sad. Nevertheless the memory revived some of his original indignant disappointment. "Why," he burst out, "a day or two after the fire I talked to your president—a great big man called Orr—"

"Stewart Orr," I said.

"Yes, Stewart Orr. Seemed a bit simple, I thought. He was all for the insurance money, and how he would build up the place just like it was. That was silly. That old Schloss, as they called it, was as ugly and inconvenient a horror as I have ever seen. All the same, I didn't let on that we would dispute the claim. I just told him how to make out a claim and I said I could collect it the next day. When I came back Orr had gone, and there was an odd sort of Britisher in his place. Spoke like a book and said there wouldn't be any claim on the company, and so"—here he gave a bad imitation of the British manner of speaking— "he would not trouble me to stay around, thanks awfully."

For one mad moment I thought of telling him the whole truth, but quickly and wisely I suppressed that desire. It was a psychological urge common, I understand, to those who have committed crimes. And besides, Joe Fletcher was not bound by any seal of the confessional. His indignation subsided and to my relief he got to talking of other things. On his professional experiences of crooks and expert arsonists, he was quite interesting, but remembering what Lionel Broadbent had said on the night of the fire, I shivered a little. If Helen had remained silent and had not told her father, we two might still have been in jail. The law takes a very unfavorable view of arson.

After midnight my fellow traveler's reminiscences dried up and he began to doze. I was wide awake. I can never sleep on a plane, and our conversation set my mind racing over the events, now more than ten years old, which had led to my first meeting with Joe Fletcher.

As it happened, I knew more of the whole story of the fire at Arcadia than anyone else. About a month afterwards Arthur Norris said to me, "Peter, you're a historian. You're not likely to meet firsthand anything more exciting than recent events. Do a bit of real historical research. Record them while they are fresh and the evidence is still available."

I recoiled at that proposal. "But," I protested, "I could never dare to print it."

"I didn't say print, I said record. And if you feel that way, just leave the record to Arcadia to be published fifty years after your death, or what you will. All the same, try to find out just what did happen, and why. And do it now."

I took part of his advice. I did collect the facts and link them up; but I did not compile any formal history. But it meant that I came to know quite a lot of the odd chain of cause and event which ended in flame and smoke that night in May.

II

ARCADIA COLLEGE WAS FOUNDED IN 1869 BY
Otto Kaufmann. The written records of its early
days were very full, carefully arranged in leather-
bound volumes and preserved in the Muniment
Room. But these all belonged to the days of Otto's
prosperity; very little survived of the years when
Otto was struggling, and even less of his boyhood.

11

The historian had therefore to rely on the uncertain and biased memories of a few old folk who had known him as a younger man. At least it was indisputable that he was a fine specimen of the immigrant boy who made good. Certainly he made very good, originally in lumber—so the official story ran. His enemies muttered that he had profited grossly from the Civil War. Probably both versions were correct. In wartime the purveyor of essential commodities can hardly avoid making money; and Otto had been brought up in a merciless school, and profited from his education.

In my early days at Arcadia I once spent two interesting but rather fruitless months trying to gather and piece together the evidence for an article on *The Early Years of Otto Kaufmann*. I did succeed in establishing at least an outline. The family came from Hanover in Germany, and were at one time dependents of a certain Baron von Knypheim, who preserved a faded stuffy feudalism. He lived in a vast castle, built in the mid eighteenth century, and ruled paternally over a little barony of about ten square miles, entirely self-sufficient with the tenant farmers, laborers, shepherds, carpenters, coopers, and other necessary craftsmen and their families—about three thousand souls in all. The Baron was a man of few ideas; his pleasures were simple and gross; and his temper was uncertain. He insisted on religious observance, and all his subjects were required to attend the local Lutheran church twice each Sunday. The general state of culture in the barony of Knypheim was low.

To this community Karl Kaufmann, Otto's father, was appointed schoolmaster. An unhappy choice, for he was infected with the free-thinking and liberal notions of the late eighteenth century. Karl had, moreover, an unjustifiably high regard for his own wisdom and culture, and a contempt for his simpler neighbors; and he soon developed a feeling of intense grievance against the world, and his employer, which he expressed tactlessly and vituperatively. When some of his choicer remarks were reported to the Baron, he sent for the schoolmaster and stormed at him with such terrifying rage that Karl gathered his few possessions and fled hastily to America where he hoped for a better life. With him he took his wife and Otto, their only child, then aged ten. These early years were important for an understanding of Otto's development. Many of the ideas which he embodied in his college did in fact stem from his boyhood memories of the red-faced Baron's little kingdom.

Otto loathed both his parents. Karl's culture was quite shallow and he was a man of limited intelligence, with simple and romantic notions; but at home he was a grim disciplinarian, and he made little Otto the scapegoat for his own failures. There was thus never any kind of sympathy between Otto and his father and even less with his mother, who merely echoed her better half, and seems to have been a stupid, sniveling woman. Life for the Kaufmanns in their adopted fatherland was hard and disappointing. Karl found the lack of culture in the New World even more depressing than in the Old; and he never learned to speak English with any kind of fluency. I could discover no trace either of Karl or of his wife after 1827; but by that time Otto had run away from home.

Young Otto prospered. He was hard-working and intelligent; and he soon had the good fortune to find employment with a middle-aged fellow German with a promising business in lumber. His employer was a widower, cared for by his only daughter, a sweet blonde girl named Emma. Otto was the perfect apprentice. At the age of twenty-two, with the full approval of her papa, he married Emma, and ultimately succeeded to the business. Thereafter his progress was rapid.

Otto and Emma were childless. This was the one real disappointment of an otherwise harmonious marriage, for Emma adored children. But perhaps it was better so, for under Emma's influence Otto conceived such softhearted notions about children and the way they should be brought up, that they would have ruined any child of their own. Had they lived two or three generations later, they would have been regarded as enlightened progressives; but in the 1840's their ideas seemed dangerously soft and unrealistic.

When Otto had made his pile, which was quite considerable even for days when millionaires were unhampered by trade unions, income taxes, or other hindrances to free enterprise, he bought a vast estate in New Hampshire; and in the center he built a colossal German-style mansion in incredibly bad taste, full of heavy woodcarving, pine paneling, and crude ugly tile work. He had hardly finished this monument to his own industry when his Emma, in the medical phraseology of the time, "went into a decline."

Emma, who must have been quite a lovable person, accepted the inevitable with perfect resignation, but she was greatly troubled for her Otto, whom she had mothered and babied for more than forty years. Without her he would be lost, and especially now that he was no longer interested in making money. She deliberately planned to give him a new interest in life which would distract him from brooding when she was gone.

"Otto, my dear," she said to him in her simple way, "what are you going to do with this great house and all our money when we don't want it any more?"

Otto was a realist in his own affairs, but he never quite dared to face ultimate realities.

"I don't know, my duckling," he answered sadly. "I just don't know."

Thereupon she outlined her plan. They had often dreamed about what they would do if they had children. Now he could have hundreds of children. In other words, let him use all this money and the estate to found a college where the young might acquire learning in an atmosphere of joy and freedom.

The idea was not entirely new to Otto. All along, in his few moments of leisure, he had been secretly dreaming this version of himself as a kind of Colossus of educational reform. When Emma died he made the dream a reality, a vast memorial to a happy marriage.

In his old age he became very sentimental. Like his more famous compatriot, Heinrich Schliemann, Otto had an amateur's love of the ancient classics; and he conceived notions of liberty which he had certainly not tested in his experience, for as an employer he was notoriously hard. But once the zest for success paled, he seemed to revert to a genial benevolence which his former employees called dotage. He brooded long over his college; it was to be a perfect Arcadia where "the nymphs and fauns play together in the green woods." Seemingly, his knowledge of mythology did not extend to the most popular of the games played by nymphs and fauns.

Thus eventually, on May Day 1869, Arcadia College was ceremoniously opened with bands, pomp, and oratory in the grotesque limestone mansion which Otto Kaufmann had built.

Otto succeeded partly by relentless hard work, but even more because he had a real genius for organization. He loved details, plans, and prospectuses. So he drew up a constitution for his college with some quite unusual clauses. Moreover, for one who started with but small book learning, he was very well read, and in educational matters surprisingly modest and humble—which is unusual for a self-made millionaire. He sought the advice of those most likely to be good guides. His correspondence with distinguished scholars, men of letters and philosophers, both British and American, was considerable. It filled eleven volumes and was by far the most interesting section of the early records in the Muniment Room. The collection included three very sensible letters from Emerson, one from Matthew Arnold which showed complete ignorance of what could be expected of an American college in the 1860's, and one from Thoreau which moved Otto to add his comment: "This man understands a hut better than a college."

The distinguished correspondents were generous with advice, a little of which Otto took. Fortunately for those who later came to serve Arcadia,

17

at an early stage in the planning he was advised to study some of Francis Bacon's observations on education, which had an admirable effect. He was impressed by Bacon's plea that professors of learning should receive good salaries and should also have every help, encouragement, and leisure for research.

Also, having been a tyrant all his life, he planned for the widest democracy for his college. The governing body was to be a Council of Nine: three outside members, three elected faculty, and three elected senior students. But—and here the old nature showed itself—the president was to be in supreme command, with the powers of a dictator, and to hold his appointment for life; and this because Otto had chosen himself as first president. And he designed a wonderful academic robe for the state occasions. Such arrangements were possible in the 1860's.

There were other clauses. Should the president be incapacitated or absent or otherwise unable to fulfill his functions, his office passed automatically to the senior faculty member of the Council of Nine.

Otto's rule was brief. He exhausted himself by his untiring efforts over the College, and within five months of taking office he suffered a stroke which left him paralyzed and speechless for three years before he died. Meanwhile an acting presi-

dent—from Harvard—was appointed to guide the
early steps of Arcadia College. As a result, for
the first sixty years Arcadia was little different
from other small arts colleges, millionaire-
founded, except that the faculty was more distinguished and the standard of learning of the students far higher, so that it soon became a place
much coveted by ambitious young scientists and
scholars who were more interested in their studies
than in making a reputation in some larger and
more famous institution.

During the decades there was small change.
After Otto there were but three presidents, all benign dictators, who interpreted the Founder's
principles according to their own paternal notions.
The fourth president—President Ezra K. Wolter—
lived to his mid eighties. He thus outlasted several
hopeful candidates for his office, and there grew
up a kind of feeling that since he would live forever, there was no need to think of the future. But
he did die, very suddenly, in the third week of the
fall semester, leaving a leaderless College, in
nominal charge of the Dean of the Arts, who for
the last twenty-nine years had never made an in-
dependent decision and had long since lost that
ability. After three weeks, order dissolved into dis-
contented bewilderment. Clearly the Dean of the
Arts was not the right successor for the late President Wolter.

The Council of Nine met to consider the crisis. Everyone instinctively yearned for drastic change. Arcadia was suffering from senility. That was in the late 1920's when experiments were in fashion, among them the notion that young men made (or would make) great college presidents, for they would bring fresh minds to old problems. One name seemed obvious: Stewart Everard Orr.

Stewart Orr was young—not yet thirty—athletic, handsome. He was six foot three and well proportioned, energetic, dynamic, and a sociologist. But the chief asset was that he already had close affinities with Arcadia. For his doctoral dissertation—a brilliant work—he chose to write *A Study of Otto Kaufmann and His Social and Educational Ideas,* which Columbia published. Later opinion was divided whether the choice of a topic was happy chance or inspired foresight. The Council's spies reported that Dr. Stewart Orr was married; and that Enid Orr, his wife, was the domesticated type unlikely therefore to try to interfere with the affairs of the College, placid, charming, and the mother of twins—David and Helen—who were being educated according to the theories of Bertrand Russell, then popular among progressives. They did not, however, discover that Mrs. Orr's father had died in a mental hospital and that her mother committed suicide. As for Stewart Orr, above all, he was as yet uncontaminated by administrative experience.

Thus it came to pass that Stewart Orr was chosen fifth president of Arcadia, and being soaked in the Kaufmann ideals he determined to make Arcadia the fulfillment of the Founder's vision. Orr was still an idealist or—as his jealous and disappointed rivals put it—an adolescent. He believed, genuinely, in liberty untrammeled by rules.

As he anticipated, the first years were difficult; but President Orr was not dismayed. Opposition was to be expected from the senior professors, some of whom were older than his father. He enjoyed the fight. To those who protested against his innovations, he would reply that he was but carrying out the wishes of the Founder, and surely no member of the faculty would wish otherwise. Gabriel Mancini, the physics professor—a man of international reputation—blasphemously retorted that old Otto was an ass in educational matters. President Orr was unruffled. He could afford to wait till Mancini should find employment elsewhere more attractive, which he did by the end of the year, for there was keen competition to allure him away. President Orr's speech at the valedictory dinner was superb, and intended as much for other malcontents as for Mancini. In words of heart-warming eulogy of the departing physicist he subtly conveyed his own sense of relief at the prospect. And throughout he continued to smile. Orr was a perpetual smiler. When the novelty wore off, irreverent students nicknamed him "Cheese."

By the end of five years Arcadia was transformed. By threes and fours the older faculty members dispersed unhappily to other campuses whence they looked back on the changes with sour prophecies of doom to come. They even said harsh things of the Kaufmann ideals, and harsher of the young President. But the President continued to smile, as well he might; he had never dreamed that the opposition would melt so quickly or so easily. And for every vacancy, he was besieged by a score or more of eager applicants.

On the whole President Orr chose his team wisely. As he became experienced in interviewing candidates for appointment, he developed a kind of ritual of initiation. He would seat the applicant in an easy chair facing the window of his impressive office. Then after a short pause, as if in silent prayer, he uttered a brief but moving account of Otto Kaufmann and his ideals. Thence he would expand on his own interpretation of the creed, and how he was in process of making it a reality. At this point the candidate was asked whether he agreed with the Orr interpretation and could adapt himself wholeheartedly to a community so different from any he had as yet encountered.

Occasionally an unwary candidate would hint at reservations. The President continued to smile but the light faded from his eager eyes and the conversation was turned aside into more general matters until the candidate was genially dismissed to return to the place whence he came, and to await a letter regretting that there was as yet no vacancy in Arcadia exactly suitable to his particular gifts.

The cannier candidate, who lacked such scruples, or who had had the better sense to conceal them, was then quizzed about his own theories and notions of teaching and learning, and so led into the crucial question: "If you had your choice, would you prefer to be a teacher or a researcher?" The correct answer was "Both." To which the reply was: "Good. You are right. Each activity stimulates the other. Good. Good."

The light in the President's eye grew brighter; and he would add, "From men who join us here at Arcadia, I look for leaders, inspiring leaders, not cattle drovers. For men whose achievement and personality are so vivid and compelling that even the dullest student will catch fire."

When the candidate had reached this stage he was safe—so long as he refrained from asking the wrong questions.

All this was very flattering to a young assistant professor, desperate for better pay and a chance to get on with his own frustrated research; and his joy at receiving the letter of appointment was ecstatic, for Orr was an impressive personality. Those who said that he was just a smiling hypocrite were unjust. He did genuinely believe in the Kaufmann ideal, and he had the instincts of a scholar. If he was also attracted to those who would be willing followers rather than active critics, that was but part of his prudent simplicity. He was looking for disciples, not critics.

By President Orr's sixth year, Arcadia, at least among young and eager graduates, had become a symbol of academic paradise.

So I found it on a sunny morning late in April when I was invited to visit the Chairman of the Department of History and to meet the President and other members of the faculty. For the past four years I had been teaching at the Detroit College of Adult Education in a grimy building, once the home of a tycoon but now decayed. Fifteen hours each week, mostly in the evening, I held classes for tired teachers, and each week I read and commented on fifty of their dreary assignments. Only by the grimmest grind had I been able to complete my book on William Godwin and his idealistic theories of political and social justice, which Jeffrey, the history man at Arcadia, found exciting.

I was thus preconditioned to see the best in Arcadia; and it was very good. The campus was concealed within three thousand acres of hilly woodland, cut in two by a swift shallow river, running over stones, with good trout fishing in the pools, so I was told. Otto's original mansion, now converted into the administration building, with offices and private laboratories for a few very special researchers, was surrounded by buildings, discreetly harmonized in matching limestone. The student body, to my thinking, was just right—about nine hundred in all, of whom about a third were women—housed in small homely dormitories, each with its own loyalties. There were good modern houses for the faculty scattered round the perimeter.

I was particularly interested in the housing, for —if I should get the appointment—I planned to get married at once. Here too Otto had designed well and wisely. There were private houses for the married, graded in sizes according to the number of the children in the family, each with its own garden and lawn. And for each of the bachelors a small cottage or bungalow—Otto had inevitably called it a "hermitage"—with a good-sized living room, a small study, and a bedroom, all very comfortably furnished. Elderly women were hired to do the cleaning and the occupants were expected to dine together in the Triclinium, which was

Otto's picturesque name for the faculty dining room in the Student Union. Naturally the place was more usually known as the Trink. All the same it was a comely and large chamber, modeled, more or less, after the hall in an Oxford college.

The library was excellent for so small a place; and there were the usual clubs, stadium, classroom buildings, and the rest. The most noticeable feature of the place was its complete isolation. It was a self-sufficient community, seemingly cut off from the world. Linton, the nearest town, was seven miles away. After Detroit this was perfect.

Jeffrey came into the town and met me at the bus depot. Then he drove me to his house and we talked on professional matters. He said pleasant things about my book which he had read with care, for he took me up on several small points. It was months since I had been able to talk about my own special interests with anyone who had expert knowledge and who spoke the same language. We discussed the teaching of history and its purposes and methods. A most stimulating morning. Then he brought in half a dozen seniors; they were friendly, well informed, and inquiring.

After lunch we crossed the campus to Otto's great limestone mansion—known officially as the Schloss—mounted the stone staircase, and entered the great entrance hall. We gazed round at the pine paneling, and the glaring tiles in the enormous fireplace; and then at the life-size portrait of Otto Kaufmann, benign, bewhiskered, wearing that peculiarly ugly black frock coat which was the mark of respectability and opulence in 1869. It was a full-length portrait, reverently and discreetly illuminated, showing Otto standing with the foundation deeds of his college clasped to his bosom in his left hand, with the right pointing vaguely to the mansion in the background. Beneath on the mantelpiece stood an ornate bronze vase.

"This," said Jeffrey in the manner of a professional guide, "is the heart of Arcadia."

I said nothing, for I found it difficult to show enthusiasm for a chamber so utterly tasteless.

"The portrait," he went on, "is that of Otto Kaufmann, our founder. A very great man. In the urn beneath are mingled the ashes of Otto Kaufmann and his beloved wife, Emma."

I glanced at him curiously; for his words were toneless, and I was uncertain whether he was sincere or ironic. Best, I thought, at this stage not to inquire. So I commented merely, "A fine example of portrait painting of that period." Adding, "I had not realized that cremation had occurred that early in this country."

After a few moments of silent reverence, Jeffrey led me up the great wooden stairs with their elaborately carved bannisters to the gallery above, and so along to the President's office. He knocked and we entered. The room was impressive, very different from the usual sterile neatness of presidential offices. The furniture was old-fashioned—heavy stuffed leather chairs, and a huge mahogany desk. The walls from top to bottom were lined with books, the right kind of books, and the room had the right kind of smell, a mixed aroma of good tobacco and old leather bindings.

President Orr came forward.

"This," said Jeffrey, "is Dr. Peter Lowe from Detroit. It is his first visit to Arcadia. Dr. Lowe is the author of that very interesting book about William Godwin."

The President sized me up. "I look forward to a most interesting talk with Dr. Lowe," said he. "I found his book quite fascinating."

Jeffrey withdrew. To my gratified surprise a copy of the book lay on President Orr's desk, and I found that he really had read it, for he asked me whether I thought that Godwin had in any way influenced Otto Kaufmann in his thinking. There were some very close parallels between the Kaufmann code, as he understood it, and the original *Inquiry Concerning Political Justice*. And he took up the book and read the passages aloud.

"It could be," said I, "but Godwin's ideals, his notion that man is essentially rational, was very much in the air at the beginning of the nineteenth century. Before I could answer your question, I would need to look more closely into the early records of Otto's correspondence with liberal thinkers of his day."

"Do I understand," asked the President eagerly, "that you have already made some study of Otto Kaufmann?"

"A little," I answered. "I have heard so much about Arcadia that naturally I wanted to know something of its history."

The President beamed approval. This zeal of mine was not, however, hypocrisy, but rather plain common sense. Fortunately I had been forewarned about President Orr's enthusiasms, and the ritual and its dangers. William Godwin's notions were still quite exciting, even to a rather jaded graduate of the twentieth century; for the young men of his own generation they must have been heady stuff; they made Wordsworth and Shelley quite wild. But except in his odd relations with women—and there was nothing particularly philosophical in that—Godwin never had any chance of trying out his ideas in actual practice; and in later life, he was—as all his enemies so triumphantly point out—a very poor advertisement for his own doctrine. Otto Kaufmann at least founded a real society on similar lines, even if he did not live to see it at work. As usually happens, his immediate successors jettisoned the Founder's doctrine and reverted to accepted convention; but now that was all changed, and under President Orr I would be able to observe how a free society actually functioned.

I was certainly making a good start. After a few further comments, the formal initiation began. President Orr's opening words, to my suppressed amusement, were a direct verbatim quotation from the concluding chapter of his dissertation. Fortunately it seemed not to have occurred to the President that my knowledge of Otto might have come principally from his own publication.

In theory at least I agreed with Otto's notions; and I was certainly impressed with President Orr. In spite of his critics, the man had a touch of greatness, and the famous smile was charming. At first meeting I liked him; it would be exhilarating to serve under a president who was almost of my own generation; for at that time President Orr was in his mid-thirties, still very handsome. Ten years earlier he must have looked like Michael Angelo's David. Ten years later he became regrettably paunchy.

I thus passed the test satisfactorily. I was careful to ask only the right questions. I parted hopefully, and I went back to my tired teachers, finding the atmosphere of my drab classroom even more oppressive. After two weeks' anxious waiting, the letter arrived inviting me to join the Department of History as an associate professor at a salary even better than I had hoped; and as for the teaching—six hours a week to be spent in whatever manner I chose, and the promise of every kind of encouragement for my research.

I took the letter along to my chairman. He read it with raised eyebrows and handed it back.

"We can't hope to match that offer," he said. "I suppose you'll accept."

"I should be a fool to refuse."

"Perhaps," he replied without enthusiasm.

"Why not?" said I. "The place is a scholar's paradise."

He was silent a bit. Then he remarked, "Paradise was fine, till the serpent got in."

"It hasn't yet," I replied rather tartly, for his reaction was irritating.

"It will. It will."

He went silent again. Then he said, "We shall be sorry to lose you." Another pause. "If ever you want to come back, there will be a place for you."

I made no reply, for his words seemed just foolishness. All the same his attitude was chilling, like a cold wind on a sunny afternoon in the swimming pool.

III

THOSE FIRST YEARS AT ARCADIA, WHICH WERE also the first years of my marriage, were the happiest I ever spent, and my admiration for old Otto and for Stewart Orr grew steadily. It was an ideal community, quite small. There were at that time fewer than eighty on the faculty, and there were no dominating faculty wives, and no feuds or factions. This, to some extent, was one happy result of the Kaufmann ideal. If a man wanted to profess himself a Communist, no one tried to stop him. We had a few with the zeal for a martyr's crown and halo—or whatever corresponds to a halo with Communists; but when no one resented their right to free expression, they soon lost all zeal to convert the campus.

As was proper we had our share of campus characters of whom the most notable was Lionel Broadbent, Professor of Greek and Latin, one of the few of the senior staff who survived the Orr revolution. Lionel, more generally known as Socrates because of his untidy appearance and ironic wisdom, had old-fashioned notions of education and an utter and quite irrational contempt for all scientists. Years ago he had come from England as a visitor to Arcadia, and there he remained. There were—so the knowing said—reasons. He was a high-church Anglican whose marriage many years ago had fallen apart. Divorce was against his principles, and he fled from a disastrous situation.

When I first came to know him, he was in his middle fifties, short (the English would have called him "tubby"), with a sarcastic tongue and a detached outlook, one who always took a contrary side in any discussion. Among the students he was reputed the toughest of all professors, a hard taskmaster but genial outside the classroom and always very good company. Moreover, he seemed omniscient. But he had no soft notions about liberty. "You came here to learn," he would say to his classes. "If you are so foolish as to come to me, you will learn." Those who opted for his courses certainly did learn, though it took them some time to appreciate his ruthless pedantic determination for accuracy. All this was a survival of rigid early training in the classics at an English Public School and from his old tutor at Oxford.

Stewart Orr would gladly have aided Broadbent's departure. From time to time he would even mention other places of learning where (so he had ascertained) his great talents would have wider opportunities. Lionel rebuffed his hints with open amusement. "Awfully good of you, President, to suggest it. But I am a bit old to want to move. Unless of course you want to fire me," he added maliciously.

At this President Orr smiled gently and replied, "Of course not, Professor Broadbent. But I sometimes wonder whether you are not finding the innovations at Arcadia somewhat uncongenial to a man of your antecedents."

And Lionel laughed. He was the one man who was quite impervious to the President's smile, and quietly defied his innovations. He treated Orr as if he were a brilliant but eccentric student who should never be taken quite seriously. When one of his colleagues expressed wonder that he could endure the changes in Arcadia, Lionel replied with unusual solemnity, "Really, I am very fond of this place. The Cheese will go the way of all flesh, and sooner than most. Meanwhile someone must uphold standards of sanity."

If these words were ever carried to President Orr, he made no sign. Probably they were, for he had his informers, notably one Robert Medley (officially known as assistant to the President), our campus gossip. Not that Broadbent was ever disloyal or a rebel; what he disapproved of, he just ignored. And no one could deny that he was a brilliant teacher, profoundly learned in a humane kind of way. And, to add to the President's difficulty, Broadbent was respected by his colleagues, who regularly elected him as one of their representatives on the Council of Nine. Nor did it add to Orr's comfort that Lionel saved him from a bad blunder in the first serious trouble of his regime.

Orr's appointments were usually sound, but for some reason never discovered, he invited a broken-toothed philosopher named Sneap to join our community. Sneap was an unpleasant person, harsh-voiced and arrogant; and he evolved a creed of naked individualism. He was one of Orr's worst mistakes, for he carried the Kaufmann creed to its illogical end.

The crisis broke when Sneap chose to expound

his own theory of liberty in a senior course on Social and Political Ideas of the Twentieth Century. In a state of ideal liberty, so he claimed, the individual fulfills his own personality. "Liberty means that I am the center of my universe. Whatever aids me to achieve my own end is therefore my good."

Sneap's relations with his students were jagged. He cowed the timid and roused the aggressive. When he began to reveal this doctrine in his classroom, he was taken up by one of his more truculent seniors, who demanded that he illustrate the thesis more closely. Said the youth, "Professor, if I am free to do just what is to my advantage, then I can ignore all moral law."

Sneap looked at him with contempt. "There is no moral law, as you call it. What is called moral law is either outmoded social convention or mere superstition."

The class gasped.

"But what about social relationships? Wouldn't it make it impossible if everyone just went his own way, regardless of everyone else?"

"All life is difficult," Sneap replied sententiously. "And brutal," he added. "If the other man gets in my way, then I push him aside. It is up to him to keep out of my way. That is the way things are in life, as you will one day find out."

The student, roused by Sneap's attitude and by

the sudden tenseness in the class, was encouraged to go on.

"Then that means that if a prof gets in my way, I would be justified in pushing him out of my way?"

"You would."

"And I would be justified in trying to make him do what I want?"

"Yes." But it was a very contemptuous "yes."

"Well, what I want from you is an A grade and you always give me a B."

The class laughed. Sneap was irritated, but the cross-examination went on.

"If what you say is true, I would be justified in cheating in an examination or getting someone else to write my assignments for me."

Sneap was tripped in his own logic, but instead of pulling back or treating his questioner lightly, he sneered. "Of course you are, if you can get away with it. And I am justified in smashing you if you try it—"

"Provided you can prove it?"

"I shall find out, be sure of that, my fine young friend."

Only one of Sneap's kind would ever get bogged down in such an argument in his own classroom. Unfortunately he loathed students as much as they loathed him.

Next day, inevitably, the student paper—*The*

Arcadia News—featured a sensational account of the exchange, with a heavy banner heading: PROF SNEAP O.K.'S CHEATING.

This was the first time that we ever saw Orr worried. The system effectively dealt with social rebels by giving them nothing to rebel against. Occasionally a girl would get herself into trouble, but then Orr would point out to the indignant parents that since they knew the traditions of Arcadia, they, not he, were responsible if their home training had not fitted their daughter for a life of freedom.

Sneap's case was different. If he stuck to this attitude, it would produce chaos in the intellectual standards on which we prided ourselves. Obviously there were limits to liberty; but how to reconcile the theory with the facts of life?

The President sent for Sneap and confronted him with *The Arcadia News:* was this an accurate account of the incident? Sneap read it disdainfully and replied that it was as accurate as could be expected of students. The President pointed out, very patiently, that such views, however theoretically justified, could in practice have the most unfortunate repercussions. But perhaps Professor Sneap in the heat of argument had said more than he intended or expressed it unfortunately.

Sneap was too crass to take this way out of his difficulty. Instead he blustered. He even quoted certain of the President's own written words. If they meant what they said, then he—Sneap—could say just what he pleased in the classroom. He was not denying the Kaufmann code; it was President Orr who apparently did not believe what he preached. The tone of the discussion became shriller and was even heard outside. Hereupon Medley, thinking it prudent to enter as if with a problem of administration, caught the last exchanges. He was just in time to hear Sneap cry out, "I am well within my rights. The constitution of Arcadia allows every professor complete freedom in his own teaching. I shall say just what I please."

President replied coldly, "You would do well, Professor Sneap, to reread the whole of the constitution. There are other clauses which you have apparently overlooked. We will continue this conversation when I have considered my course of action."

Sneap withdrew. Had Medley not been present, he would have slammed the door behind him. Orr said nothing to Medley; but Medley was not so reticent when he next came into the Faculty Club.

As it happened, Sneap was wrong, for by Otto's original constitution the President had absolute powers if not of life and death, at least of summary dismissal, of any member of the faculty. Nevertheless, it was all very worrying. Not only was Sneap openly truculent, he defied Orr to dismiss him. And if Orr threw him out, then he would appeal to the Association for the Protection of Academic Rights.

President Orr in his perplexity even took his trouble to that bulwark of academic freedom. He went down to New York and laid the problem before the Association's experts who protect the liberties of unconventional professors. He asked them for advice. He showed them clauses in the constitution dealing with the presidential powers. "If," said he, "Professor Sneap is dismissed, it will be because he proclaims views which are academically impossible. He threatens me that he will appeal to you. What will be your attitude?"

The experts were very guarded. By instinct they were opposed to autocratic presidents. They replied coldly that their action would necessarily depend on the terms of Sneap's dismissal. The constitution of Arcadia was ancient; in the sixty years and more since its foundation, the rights of academic teachers had been greatly advanced. If Professor Sneap were to be dismissed summarily solely because his views were obnoxious to the President, then obviously Professor Sneap was being denied academic freedom. In any case, he must be given the fullest opportunity of publicly answering any charges that might be made against him; and if necessary he should be allowed counsel. They concluded coldly by observing that they had not hitherto been confronted with this particular problem. They could not forecast their attitude until the appeal had actually been made. If President Orr expected any other answer, he was even simpler than his enemies supposed.

It was now the second week in December and in a few days students and faculty would be departing for the Christmas holidays. On his return to Arcadia, the President found that the Sneap incident had blown up almost into a riot. He received phone calls and anonymous letters, all demanding that he do something before the semester ended.

The Council of Nine was summoned. The President, feeling very unsure of himself, laid the problem before his advisers. Eight of them urged him to use his constitutional powers and to eject Sneap from the campus with every mark of ignominy. The three student members especially were bitter. They were so indoctrinated with the notion that Arcadia was better and stricter in its standards than any comparable college that they repudiated Sneap's doctrine even more hotly than the outside members. They also disliked him so heartily as a man that they were eager for his public humiliation.

To Orr's annoyance, Lionel Broadbent sat through the proceedings without a word. At last the President turned to him and with some asperity remarked, "We have not yet heard Professor Broadbent's socratic views."

Lionel looked at the others. At last he made quite a speech (duly reported by Medley, who was the official secretary of the Council).

"Let us show a little common sense in this matter," he began. "First, we are now in the last days of the winter term. I have long observed that no one in our teaching profession is ever quite sane at this time of the year. We are all tired after thirteen weeks of teaching and learning. The days grow colder and darker. We are at the lowest ebb of the year. Our tempers are frayed and we are incapable of sound judgment. And that applies not only to Sneap but also to this Council."

He paused for comments. No one spoke. So he went on:

"Apart from that, use your imaginations. What will happen if Sneap is thrown out? He will appeal to the A.P.A.R. They will send up a committee of investigation which will then publish a written report. On paper Sneap will inevitably seem to be a martyr. Arcadia, the professed home of academic freedom, has denied the most elementary freedom of opinion to one of its members! How awful! What will not appear in the report is that Sneap is a nasty little runt who has only himself to thank for his troubles. And that's usually true of most of these academic rows. Nine times out of ten a man is thrown out not because of his views or his politics but because he is just impossible. That fact never appears, for that kind of man can always make out a good case—on paper.

"Of course, it's not always the man; there are some presidents too who should never have been appointed."

President Orr ignored the insult—if it was an insult, for he could never be quite sure of the inner meaning of Lionel's remarks. Lionel went on.

"We are not really concerned with Sneap's views, though he would never have held them, let alone talked about them with students, unless he had been such an overwhelming ass.

"Let this cool over the Christmas holidays. Either Sneap will do something so outrageous that he will destroy himself, or else he will perhaps learn sense when he cools off; and then he may realize that he has made an ass of himself. Personally, I doubt it.

"So, Mr. President, if you want my opinion, then I suggest that you do not put this to the vote, but just adjourn the discussion for three months and see what happens in the interval."

So it was left.

Lionel was soon proved right but not in the way he had anticipated. Sneap left for California, and being still in a vile bad temper, he drove recklessly, and demonstrated his notions of liberty on the expressway until he met another like himself. Neither survived the head-on crash.

President Orr was badly shaken by this episode. When he heard the news, he suffered severe feelings of guilt, as if he were Sneap's murderer. But apart from Sneap he was beginning to see a flaw in the creed. Logically it was difficult to counter Sneap's doctrine. And if the theoretical liberty of the individual led to general cheating and a breakdown of all restraints, then chaos was come again.

Nor did he recover his balance until he had thought up a solution, which was quite brilliant. He proclaimed that henceforward all grades, and final examinations leading thereto, should be abolished.

Soured senior professors—the few who still survived—complained that students needed the stimulus of competition; and besides how could a student's ability be judged unless it was tested and graded? The younger members were less hostile; it would relieve them of a heavy chore.

President Orr replied with a patient superior smile that good teaching was stimulus enough, and that, surely, was the real intention of our Founder. He also evolved a new principle to counter any ill-timed logical interpretation of the code which he called "Intuitional Control." "Liberty," said he, "is the soul of Arcadia, but liberty tempered always by intuitional control." Intuitional control proved very useful in dealing with awkward people. Since the President was the final judge of what was and what was not desirable, he could always discourage discordant views by an appeal to intuitional control. Other people called it common sense or even just normal decency.

Lionel Broadbent's reactions were typical. When the decree abolishing grades was published, he made a few carefully chosen remarks to his classes.

"Our most estimable President, with the enthusiasm of youth—and its inexperience—has abolished grades and tests. It is our duty at all times to obey constituted authority, as St. Paul so rightly tells us. And where, Miss Hughes," he asked one of his flightier students, "does St. Paul tell us that?"

Miss Hughes blushed and was silent.

Broadbent looked at her with pitying curiosity; and when no reply was forthcoming, he went on. "No matter. If ever you are persuaded to read your Bible—a most interesting volume, I may add—you may eventually discover. But—as I was saying—since our excellent President has decreed the abolition of grades and tests, we hereby abolish them. Hereafter, therefore, the results of your labors, to which I have hitherto, but rarely, appended the sign alpha (or A), will be noted as 'excellent.' For the letter B, plus or minus, which is the normal grade of most of you, I shall conclude my comments with 'good' or 'fairly good.' What used to be graded gamma—or in our illiterate age C—will be denoted 'fair.' And for the rest, the comment will be 'unsatisfactory' or just 'bad.' I add, moreover, that like the unfortunate subjects of King Rehoboam, henceforward, you will find my little finger to be thicker than my father's loins. In plainer language, the standard demanded of you will be considerably higher. Now we understand each other."

The results of this change surprised both Orr and Broadbent. Broadbent's courses became steadily more popular. Seemingly his students preferred the greater severity. Orr was baffled. Lionel merely remarked that some of the students of Arcadia had more sense than he had anticipated.

Life at Arcadia returned to its normal euphoric tranquillity.

IV

THE TROUBLE ORIGINALLY STARTED IN THE
Baconian Club. Most colleges have this kind of
club—a small group of those interested in research, who meet periodically to hear and discuss
a paper given by one of the members who are
the elite of any faculty. In our club it was a good
tradition that all papers should be intelligible to

47

the whole audience; too often researchers—and this applies especially to all who hold themselves to be men of science or exact learning—are so keen to display their own profundity that their reports are written in a learned technical jargon quite meaningless to anyone outside their narrow speciality. It is also a common experience that a small club is dominated by three or four members who tend to monopolize debate; and sometimes quite violent rivalries develop. So it was in our Baconian Club, which used to meet on the last Saturday of every month in the house of one of the members.

The Baconian Club was one of Stewart Orr's innovations, and he attended regularly. It helped him to get to know his more distinguished colleagues, and to keep in touch with the general morale of Arcadia. He was true to his principles, and his presence encouraged rather than restrained the widest discussion on the most delicate topics.

Naturally, Lionel Broadbent was one of our stalwarts, and a great trial to the more single-minded scientists, for he would quiz them in his socratic manner. And having a nimbler wit and tongue, he could be very provoking. Moreover, he was often quite unfair in his criticisms. At the same time he was very good for the club, for he stood for ancient—even if outmoded—values in a changing world.

Lionel's opposite was Calvin Chapman, one of Orr's most successful importations. He was fair-skinned, tall, thin and a little stooping, with thick sandy hair which he rumpled when worried. He was a vigorous walker, and his one extravagance was a large expensive sports car. Being a bachelor, he could indulge in this kind of luxury. His hobby was the earlier history of the Indian troubles, on which he was quite an authority.

He was also one of the very select band who were allotted an office in the Schloss. Calvin was a young biologist who was making some quite sensational experiments in the crossing of species. By some method which he never divulged, he had apparently broken down the natural barriers which usually make one species impervious to another. There were vague suggestions of radiation and frequencies and such things, which I never could understand. The results were spectacular. He started with insects and evolved hybrids which astonished the entomologists, though mere historians and literary men, who are inclined to classify insects into bugs which sting and bugs which don't, were only mildly interested. When he succeeded in producing a creature which was a cross between a cat and a rabbit, even the least scientific of us was amazed.

These freaks Chapman exhibited to the Baconian Club to illustrate a paper on "Some Experiments in Miscegenation." But he asked us to keep it confidential until he had perfected the method and had probed more deeply into the greater principles involved.

Calvin Chapman, like so many of the generation of scientists hatched during the 1920's and 1930's, was a brash atheist and a voluble talker, all the same a very lovable man. He was quite fond of Lionel as a person but found him maddening as a colleague, especially when Lionel would claim that there were depths and mysteries in life which could be perceived by the sensitive but never analyzed. To Calvin such talk was nonsense. Unless a thing could be analyzed, categorized, tabulated, and experimented upon, it could not exist. He had no use for nuances, intuitions, and mysteries. He had his limitations.

Calvin's paper impressed the scientists, but it was too technical for me. From what I remember of it—it was never published—his ultimate aim was to discover the principle of life. Life on earth, so he theorized, had first started through a discharge of lightning which produced some kind of electrical activity, and this set going the chain of being. He had some hope that his experiments might result in controlling the life factor. It was far too early to foresee what might happen, but working on his theory he had produced some surprising results.

Hereupon he opened a basket and drew forth

his specimens, extraordinary and rather repulsive creatures, with the claws and tail of a cat and the face and ears of a rabbit. There were five of them, a single litter, bred from a female rabbit.

And how, he was asked, did he ever persuade a rabbit to mate with a cat?

Calvin smiled at the naïveté of his questioner. "By the same process of artificial insemination that enables a bull to serve a thousand cows."

Lionel Broadbent was disturbed. "I have always felt repugnance at that kind of experiment. I suppose it is permissible with animals; but with humans it is frankly indecent and contrary to all natural law."

And with that fierce argument flared up.

"Why?" retorted Calvin.

"For several reasons," Lionel answered. "But I doubt whether they would appeal to you. Personally, I find it instinctively indecent."

"Whose instinct? Yours? Not mine!"

"No. I can see that. But to take it lower, it is also in the eyes of the law plain adultery, and the resulting offspring is a bastard!"

Whereupon Arthur Norris, our literary expert, a ribald man, who always loved to stir up argument, began to quote *Lear:* "Now gods, stand up for bastards." He added. "How right you are, Lionel. Did you happen to see that case in the British courts some months ago? A woman doctor got one of her patients pregnant by artificial insemination. The husband was so wild about it that he sued his wife for adultery, with the woman doctor as the guilty party. So you see, Calvin."

Calvin ignored this flippancy and replied, "I don't set so much store on adultery as you do, Lionel. You think that the world will come to an end if a man gets into bed with another man's wife."

Norris and Jeffrey looked at each other; Calvin evidently did not know of Lionel's private misfortunes. Lionel took no notice, but replied, "It happens to be forbidden in the Ten Commandments."

"What of that? What are your Ten Commandments? Primitive taboos of the Hebrews at an early stage of their development."

There was some laughter at this.

"If you reject the Ten Commandments, what do you accept as binding on human behavior?"

"Nothing!" exclaimed Chapman. But he added disarmingly, "In theory, that is, though I would certainly get pretty mad if anyone tried to commit adultery with my wife—if I had one. I might even shoot him!"

"Yes," said Lionel, "that's why adultery is discouraged. Not unreasonably, moral law is the expression of what makes for general harmony."

Someone at this point interjected with "I don't

52

quite see what all this has to do with Chapman's experiments."

"It has, quite a lot," replied Lionel. "They may be within the limits of what is—or what is not—justifiable. But he might be tempted to make experiments which are contrary to all laws, human and divine."

Calvin was roused, "You mean to say that there are limits to scientific inquiry?"

"Just that," said Lionel.

Several of the scientists murmured their dissent at such heresy.

"You scientists," retorted Lionel, "suffer from incurable pride. And pride is the first of the deadly sins, if you can imagine what they are. Because you are finding out things which have never been found out before, you think you're free of all controls. Yes, I know most of you don't believe in divine law or anything of that sort. But you are not the first people to make that mistake. Literature and history are full of the awful warnings of what happens to men who try to know things that they should not. I suggest that you reread—or read—the story of Dr. Faustus. He wanted to know forbidden things and he came to a sorry end. The Devil just picked him up by the feet and banged him against the wall till his eyes fell out. That's what will happen to some of you!"

He said it lightheartedly and there was general laughter.

President Orr was getting uneasy at this turn in the argument; it reminded him somewhat of Sneap. "I am sure," said he, judiciously, "that we may trust Professor Chapman to preserve a proper intuitional control in all his inquiries."

Calvin made no reply. Lionel muttered, "I wonder."

Soon afterward the meeting dispersed with general congratulations to Calvin for his discoveries, and his paper, and a good discussion, mingled with some irritation at Broadbent's remarks. It was after this meeting that Lionel and I had an argument which might have led to a permanent coolness. I remonstrated with him.

"You were very unfair to Calvin and the scientists at the Baconian," I protested.

"How so?" said he with bland innocence.

"Because you are denying them freedom of inquiry. And surely that is the very foundation of any civilized society, especially an academic society. Besides, you base your principles on Christian theology. And if you believe it, as you always claim you do, then the whole thing depends on free will."

"Of course," Lionel replied. "That's the real trouble: free will."

"Well, you're denying free will to Calvin and the other biologists."

"I am not. He has entire free will. But free will

means the power of choice. Of choosing whether to act or not to act."

"Right. Calvin chooses to act; and his action takes the form of producing those nasty hybrids. What's wrong in that?"

"So far nothing. All the same I don't like it."

"That's just sheer prejudice."

"Far from it, my dear Peter. I don't like it because it is verging on the forbidden."

"Forbidden? By whom?"

Lionel sighed patiently. "I would say God. But to a pure Godwinian, like yourself, I suppose that means nothing."

"Not much," I said. "I would prefer to say—if you must say it—that it is contrary to reason. And aren't you in danger of repeating the mistake the Inquisition made over Galileo? They thought his ideas contrary to the will of God and they gave him the full works. And after that they found that he was right and they were wrong; and they looked very foolish." I said that with some heat.

"Dear old Galileo!" he replied. "They always bring in Galileo whenever anyone questions science. Has it not occurred to you—as an historian—that there might have been another way of looking at it? The real reason, I suspect, why Galileo got into trouble was not because of his revolutionary theories about the way the stars behave—only half a dozen higher mathematicians could understand it anyway—nor because of his dabbling in theology, in which he was not an expert. It was a far more human reason. The old gentleman was one of those cantankerous caustic academics with a perverted sense of humor who blister everyone who won't accept his latest theories. A bit like the late and unlamented Sneap. Of course that's not the official version of the Galileo incident; but have another look at it in that light."

"Perhaps so," I admitted. "All the same I think your objections are mostly irrational prejudice. You just don't think it's quite nice to try that kind of experiment. It offends the moral sense of your grandmother!"

Lionel looked at me from under his thick eyebrows.

"You never knew my grandmother, my mother's mother, that is. She was a remarkable old lady, singularly free from prejudice, as it happens. Still, I admit your figure of speech. Let me put it another way. I believe in God as the ultimate sanction of what is right and of what is not. You believe in reason. Reason is your sanction. Where, in its turn, does your reason get its sanction?"

"From the common sense of rational men."

"Exactly," cried Lionel triumphantly. "That's what we usually call natural law—or as the estimable Orr puts it 'intuitional control.' To that extent you and I are really in agreement. We both believe in sanctions, in a kind of *ne plus ultra* or as the vulgar would say: YOU STOP HERE. My objection to Calvin is that he has no *ne plus ultra*."

"But," I protested, "what right have you to put up your STOP signs. Calvin's experiments offend your delicate sense of decency, but you don't know whether he may not make some discovery which will revolutionize our whole notion of the universe. And anyhow isn't your notion of the will of God just a grand way of saying 'I don't like this'?"

I must have said this very offensively, for Lionel refused to continue the argument, and that was unusual with him. He replied gently, "This is something that neither of us can prove. And the more you argue, the more you convince yourself that you are right and the other man is wrong, and probably wicked as well. But perhaps you will admit what is called, I believe, the pragmatic test: does it work? If Calvin's experiments lead to an ultimate increase of joy in the human race then he is right. And I am wrong."

There was no more to be said.

Two months later it was Lionel Broadbent's turn to entertain the club with a paper. Most unhappily he was inspired by Chapman's effort to counter with "Some Classical Hybrids." If he meant it as a joke, it misfired. If as a warning, it had the contrary effect. All the same it was an interesting survey, learned and witty, of the curious creatures of classical mythology—the minotaur, satyrs, the chimera, and centaurs.

When the time came for questions, Calvin examined him eagerly. "How do you suppose the Greeks ever came to invent such creatures as the minotaur and the rest?"

"There are various explanations," Lionel replied rather pedantically. "We now know from the excavations of Arthur Evans and others that a peculiarly dangerous kind of bullbaiting was practiced in ancient Crete. It was quite different from a Spanish bullfight or the cruelty of Elizabethan bullbaiting. Instead of killing the bull, athletic young men and women were trained to vault over fierce bulls and to show other feats of agility. There must have been many nasty accidents. If, as seems probable, these athletes were gathered from the Greek cities, probably by forced levy, one can see how a tradition would arise that a Cretan bull-god demanded human sacrifices. As for centaurs, they were probably invented by some tribe or people that for the first time encountered cavalry or other mounted invaders; or perhaps the legend of the centaur—if we could date its origin—may have been a scared peasant's account of his first sight of a man riding on a horse."

"What about satyrs?"

"I have no theory about satyrs, except that it may have been a picturesque way of saying that some men are like goats! I'm sorry to say 'may be' so often; but in spite of our anthropologists, professional and amateur, we just don't know."

At this Tom Cummins, one of the psychologists, interposed. "Is there really any obscurity about the origin of satyrs? If you come to think of it, each of your hybrids is a symbol of man's animal nature. The minotaur is a type of the brute killer man—the prize-fighter kind. The centaur—half man and half horse—is man the intelligent animal. And the satyr is a type of the uninhibited sexual instinct."

"To some extent I would agree," Lionel replied, "especially about satyrs. They were symbols of unrestrained lust. That is why you see them so often portrayed in wall paintings and statues in Pompeii and similar middens of iniquity."

But Calvin was eager for more information.

"Am I right in supposing that all these creatures belong to one period of Greek history, or rather prehistory?"

"Seemingly so."

"And they never bred?"

"I have never heard of satyrs breeding. Besides, they seem always to have been males."

"That's interesting! So are all my hybrids! Another thing. At the time they existed, were there any legends of unusual storm phenomena? Lightnings and the like?"

"Why, certainly. Zeus was the god of thunder and he was very free with his bolts. He wiped out the Titans that way."

Calvin sat up straight as if he had just made a wonderful discovery. "I would bet that they really existed!"

"What?"

"Why, satyrs and centaurs. There was some peculiar radioactive condition which caused abnormal fertility and these creatures were the result."

"But you need both a goat and a man to produce a satyr."

"Yes," said Calvin, "but the Greeks had quaint habits. They were not bound by your Mosaic laws."

Hereupon the psychologists took up the argument, and talked learnedly of the collective unconscious and universal symbols.

All this happened one Saturday evening. On the Monday, Calvin came round to Lionel's office to continue the conversation. He wanted fuller information and he asked where he could pursue the matter. Lionel gave him quite a long list of books. Then he asked why a biologist was so interested in a matter so far removed from his usual inquiries.

"Just an idea," Calvin replied.

Lionel was suspicious. "You're not going to try

any unholy experiments, are you? If you have that thought, I beg you to drop it. It can only lead to some awful disaster."

Calvin answered, "You and I have different creeds. You believe that the universe is controlled by a person you call God who has laid down all sorts of laws and prohibitions. I don't. I have nothing but my own intellect to guide me. To me, science is religion. I am as strongly compelled by my religion to go on trying to find out how the universe works as you are to follow your own particular set of do's and don't's. I guess that's where we differ."

"I guess it is," said Lionel.

A few days later Calvin Chapman applied for a special research grant to enable him to acquire ten she-goats. He proposed to lodge the goats in the stables which adjoined the old coach house at the extreme southwest edge of the original estate. Calvin was given his grant; and for the time the matter was forgotten.

V

AT THE BEGINNING OF HIS ELEVENTH YEAR AS president, Stewart Orr's relationship with Arcadia became closer and more personal. The twins—David and Helen—were now eighteen and both were entered as first-year students. Very rightly they chose to live in dormitories and not at home; and—a matter which Orr overemphasized—they were to be treated exactly as other students. In so small a college this was hardly possible. For my part, I have always demurred at the presence of the children of colleagues in my classes; but this may be due to hypersensitivity, or—as my psychology colleagues would say—to a sense of personal insecurity. But, in general, there was little enthusiasm to welcome Helen Orr; most of us knew her too well already.

When first they came to Arcadia, President and Mrs. Orr were much impressed with the latest theories of child education, and they determined that the twins should start life untrammeled by those inhibitions which have wrecked so many young lives. The word "no" was never heard in their home. Bathroom doors were never locked, and if the children wished to frolic with their parents in the bath, they frolicked.

The Orrs persuaded some of the faculty, who were blessed with offspring of the same age, that a school taught by someone really progressive would be a natural adjunct to Arcadia. Accordingly an expert, trained in the latest ways, was brought over from England to found and organize the venture. The name of this lady was Gwendolen Sheepshanks, an impressive Englishwoman of about thirty-six years, thickset, athletic, and commanding. On the golf course she could defeat all but three of the faculty, but she was less of a success socially. She lacked tact—but perhaps that is too harsh a criticism. Certainly she always said just what she felt, and she felt quite strongly about some of our national customs; and she was one of those women with whom one does not disagree. She would have made an admirable, though not necessarily popular, commandant in a women's army.

In her classroom Miss Sheepshanks was magnificent. She taught her little charges the full doctrine of absolute uninhibited freedom. Harsh commands and rebukes were never heard; they were never needed. Of a morning Miss Sheepshanks would gather her flock around her. Then she would say, "Now children, what shall we do today?" And each child would be encouraged to express his or her desires (as it happened there were more her's than his's; academics do seem to run rather to daughters).

"Yes, Johnnie?"

"I want substracting."

"And you, Daphne?"

"History."

"And what about Beverly?"

Beverly seemingly had no ideas.

So she would go round till one of them proposed what she had already intended.

"Geography? Stella says geography. Now, who wants geography?"

Usually the children had the sense to realize

that this was what the lawyers call a leading question, and they would pipe up in enthusiasm for geography. So geography it was that morning.

Occasionally there would be opposition, especially if the champion of the day's intention was unpopular. Miss Sheepshanks was quite ready to deal with that situation. "It is such a long time since Carol was leader. Don't you think it would be nicer if Carol is allowed to choose this morning?"

Nicer feelings usually prevailed.

The real test, however, was little Helen Orr, reputed to be utterly uncontrollable. Helen eyed Miss Sheepshanks, wondering how far she dared. Once, and quite early in the school's existence, Helen was asked the morning question, "What would Helen like to do today?" She answered insolently and emphatically, "Nothing."

"Come here, Helen dear," said Miss Sheepshanks in a very kind voice, alarmingly quiet.

Helen came. Miss Sheepshanks held her, a hand on each arm; and Helen realized that they were very firm hands.

In her kindest manner, looking Helen straight in the eyes, Miss Sheepshanks repeated the question, "What would Helen like us to do today?"

Helen sensed authority and she respected it. She replied softly, "Whatever you think best, Miss Sheepshanks." There was no further trouble.

Such were Miss Sheepshanks' powers of persuasion that her little flock made amazing progress. They were at least two years ahead of children of the same age brought up in the Linton schools. And their manners were refined and social. Everyone agreed that Miss Sheepshanks was a great asset in our secluded community, though we were careful in selecting the rest of the company when we invited her to dinner. As for Lionel, he avoided her. But that was to be expected. The English always hate each other when they meet on alien soil. Besides, he began to suspect that she had designs on his supposed bachelor status, for she made outrageous and crude attempts to attract his notice.

As Lionel never played golf and had no interest whatever in small children, the two of them would seldom in ordinary circumstances meet; but Miss Sheepshanks was persistent though hardly subtle. She wrote him little notes, asking for information on matters of myth and story. She borrowed his books, which was infuriating; for though Lionel was a generous man, he hated lending his own books, even though she always returned them quite quickly. In fact she made special visits to his cottage to return them, and usually in the evening, when she stayed chatting quite late. At first Lionel was mildly amused, but soon she became a bore, and then an agony, for Lionel had been very nicely brought up and he had never learned how to repel a persistent woman.

Finally Miss Sheepshanks made a last and desperate direct assault. Her original contract was for two years. In another ten days she would have to decide whether or not to renew it for a further two years, as indeed all the happy parents urged her. She went round to Lionel, and having seated herself solidly in his own special chair—a social lapse of the worst kind—she said that she had come for some advice on a difficult and personal problem which Dr. Broadbent alone could give her. By this time, Lionel was alarmed. In the beginning he was distantly kind, treating her as if she were the less than favorite niece of an elderly uncle. But, as was becoming clear, Miss Sheepshanks was not interested in uncles.

Campus observers were fascinated by the contest, and bets were even exchanged that Gwendolen would get her man. Sympathies were divided. Those who were irked by Lionel's irritating ways hoped, rather maliciously, that like the original Socrates he would be ensnared by a masterful woman. Others felt that since Miss Sheepshanks was so grievously handicapped by lack of every kind of feminine charm, she deserved a lucky break.

No one, not even the omniscient Medley, ever discovered just what did pass at the final meeting. Both parties were grimly reticent. Next morning Lionel was obviously shaken; he even called the lady "that damned harpy." She on the other hand hinted darkly that Dr. Broadbent, though elderly, ugly, and singularly unattractive, was, to those who came to know him intimately, lechery incarnate.

The result for Arcadia was inevitable. Miss Sheepshanks decided not to renew her contract; she would enlarge her acquaintance with the United States and try her luck elsewhere, preferably in a state where the climate was less rigorous.

So she went. Too soon we knew that she had gone.

Her successor was a charming young lady from the South, soft-voiced (you could never say that of Miss Sheepshanks), feminine, appealing, with most of the gentler qualities which her predecessor had lacked, but also without those sterner traits which seemingly were needed to cope with a score of faculty children. Uninhibited liberty, as practiced under Miss Sheepshanks' regime, quickly degenerated into nasty riotous license. Anxious parents withdrew their children and dispatched them daily by bus to continue a more conventional education at Linton. The little school closed down. Outside observers declared that the main cause of disaster was Helen Orr.

Helen was one of those children who attract and demand attention. Physically she was a throwback to one of her remoter forebears, for while Stewart Orr and his wife were notably Nordic, Helen was petite, dark-haired, dark-eyed, with that kind of skin sometimes called olive, very introverted, a child who lived inside a world of her own ("inhabited by devils," said Arthur Norris), unpredictable, moody, but given also to sudden exhibitions of quite fascinating charm. She was that way from childhood.

After the first brief encounter, Helen became a devoted follower of Miss Sheepshanks, but she despised her successor, whom in two days she reduced to public weeping. It seemed incredible that so small a person could have thought up such subtle, ingenious, and fiendish torments. At home she was intolerable. Stewart Orr, who was not much given to introspection, probably never realized the feelings of his colleagues, or that his own daughter was the worst possible advertisement of the Kaufmann creed. Enid Orr did; as was revealed on a famous occasion in the Norris household.

One Sunday afternoon Helen came over to play with the Norris children and was raising hell in the living room. Norris told her to keep quiet. He even cried out, "Don't make such a noise."

Helen defied him. "My daddy never says 'Don't.'"

He raised his voice.

Thereupon she reached over at a vase full of flowers and deliberately smashed it in the fireplace. Norris took up a thick section of the *New*

York Times, rolled it up, put the child over his knee and was about to beat her when she bit him. He dropped the paper and used his hand, hard. Helen ran home, screaming vengeance.

Arthur and his wife had quite an argument about it. She rebuked him severely for the loss of temper, but while her distress was mental, Norris himself was still feeling acute pain from little Helen's white teeth. Next morning, however, he was suffering some remorse, especially when he happened to meet Mrs. Orr as he was crossing the campus. She spoke first.

"I am afraid that you had some trouble with Helen yesterday."

"Yes," replied Norris. "I am afraid we did. I smacked her, I am sorry to say."

"What did she do?"

"She bit me."

"And you smacked her for that?"

"Yes," said Norris rather sheepishly.

Mrs. Orr smiled at him sweetly.

"Thank you," she said.

Then she added rather sadly, "I do wish that Stewart would forget his theories and lose his temper once in a while. We should all be so much happier." The close friendship of the Norrises and the Orrs (especially Enid Orr), started from this episode.

David Orr, on the other hand, was the complete

conformist and never gave trouble. When he grew up, he would be very like his father in looks. He was always superlatively good at games, and generally popular, but as he lacked his father's brain, he was not, seemingly, destined for academic greatness. He was a most attractive boy, and very well liked. More notice would have been taken of him if he could have been separated from his sister.

After the departure of the lady known as the Southern Belle, David and Helen were perforce brought up as other children. They lived at home, but Monday through Friday each week they would depart on the school bus and not be seen till late afternoon. Saturday and Sunday we realized their presence.

It was the hospitable custom of the Orrs to invite senior members of the faculty, four at a time with their wives or other partners, to dinner once each semester. These command performances could be a nightmare, depending on the unpredictable mood of their daughter, for the twins were always included in the party. When Helen was feeling benign, she was a most attractive teenager, lively and witty for her age and a good talker. Occasionally she would have a sense of the occasion and would then sit demurely silent, but using her dark eyes. More usually she was insolent, especially to her father. Once, when my wife and I were among the guests, Stewart Orr was holding forth quite brilliantly. Helen showed her boredom, first by yawning and then by fidgeting. Still her father went on. She put both her elbows on the table and remarked loudly, "Aw, Pop, I wish you'd shut up. You're all wet."

Her father beamed, as if this was a sally of quite exceptional wit. Mrs. Orr blushed. The rest of the company froze.

As she grew into adolescence Helen became a menace to our world, especially to the male students. Three at least of our seniors dropped out of school after severe mental disturbance, for Helen took a delight in tormenting boys. It made one understand why women are sometimes left strangled in motels. Behavioral experts talk about Jekyll and Hyde, or schizophrenia, or double personality. Helen's personality was quadruple. There was the usual Helen, untidy and bedraggled, with her long dark hair uncombed, her face seemingly unwashed, slouching in faded jeans, and wearing old untidy loafers on bare feet. Then there was a Helen who dressed flashily to attract boys of a kind; in that guise she was even more repulsive. But there was a third Helen who appeared in admirable good taste, smartly dressed, well groomed, perfumed and poised; and this Helen was a real beauty, even at fifteen, very regal and untouchable. More rarely there was a demure Helen, who wore sober clothes and spoke primly and seldom. The only reliable thing about her was that she played the part in which she was dressed. The real Helen— if there was one—no one ever knew.

To young men about campus she was maddening. In her demure character she would flirt violently with some sober romantic youth and lead him on to a second date when to his amazed horror she would appear as Helen the Slut. The sloppy Joes got the contrary treatment. When they had become used to her in jeans and loafers, she would invite them to come as they were to the presidential mansion, where she would condescend to them in her queenliest vesture.

All this was so very disturbing that even the President was at last made to realize that his daughter was a menace to his regime. Arthur Norris, as one who knew the Orrs best, was deputed to convey the sad fact as tactfully but firmly as could be, and to demand Helen's exile. Norris agreed, but on condition that he used his own methods of achieving the desired end. He maneuvered adroitly.

First, Mrs. Norris invited Mrs. Orr to come round to discuss a matter concerning the Faculty Women's Club. Norris joined them as if by accident. He had great respect and considerable sympathy for Mrs. Orr's quiet common sense. Ever since his trouble with Helen he realized that Enid Orr was the silent victim of her husband's theories and her

daughter's tantrums. As she was quite without any
subtlety, the direct approach was best and quick-
est. Norris came to the point at once.

"Enid," he said, "how far does Stewart know
what goes on round the campus?"

"What do you mean?"

"I mean does he know that unless something is
done about Helen quickly, there will be a revolution in the faculty?"

"Oh dear," she sighed, "is it really as bad as
that?"

"Not far off it."

"But what can be done? You know Stewart. He
won't believe anything against Helen, though she
treats him abominably."

"She ought to be sent away to some place else.
Arcadia's too small for her. She needs other interests and other people."

"For her sake or theirs?" asked Mrs. Orr bitterly.

"For neither," Norris answered, "but rather for
ours, and yours. She would be in no greater danger
than she is here. Helen will go her own obstinate
way wherever she is. And she can get into trouble
here as easily as anywhere else."

Enid Orr agreed. "I'm afraid you're right. But
how could anyone persuade either Helen or Stewart that she should go? If Stewart could be made
to see it that way, Helen would refuse to go just to

annoy her father. And I don't see any way of persuading Helen to want to go."

"It could be done, with luck," said Norris. "If you'll agree, I'll try. But say nothing to Stewart."

"Arthur, do what you can. I am nearly at the end of what I can stand."

A week later the Norrises were dinner guests with the President and Mrs. Orr. That evening Helen was in her queenly mood, as a kind of compliment to Arthur Norris, who was one of the very few people in Arcadia who had ever dared to lay hands on her. Norris waited till the end of the meal; he wanted no interruptions. Then he said,

"President, I would like to hear your opinion on a question that Professor Jeffrey and I got quite excited about a couple of days ago."

"What was the trouble?"

"No trouble, but rather a practical and theoretical matter of educational and family policy."

"That sounds interesting."

Norris went on without a glance at Helen or even a sign that he realized she was present. "Our question was this: When one's children reach a certain age—the adolescent stage when they are on the edge of complete adult responsibility—is it desirable that they stay at home, or that they go away from home as far as possible, even to a foreign country, to develop by themselves and to finish their education?"

"How did you come to discuss that?"

"Well, Jeffrey was talking about his niece, his brother's daughter, a girl of sixteen. Her parents sent her to some kind of finishing school in Paris and she is having a wonderful time."

"Do you agree with that?" asked President Orr sharply.

"It is a purely academic question with us for the next five years. But so far as I feel now, I would need a lot of persuading to send any child of mine away to Paris; though I suppose it rather depends on what the word Paris connotes. All the same our feeling is that the proper place for a child is the home."

"You are right," the President commented. "Nothing can compensate for the lost years of home life, especially when the child is in the late teens."

Helen exchanged glances with David, fortunately not perceived by her father, for they were disrespectful.

The President became quite emphatic. "I would never encourage, or even permit, a child of mine to travel abroad by herself. Never."

Helen ignored this pronouncement and leaned over the table.

"What sort of place in Paris?" she asked. "Is it really a school?"

Norris replied, "It can hardly be a school, as I

understand school. The girls seem to have very few rules. They do have classes where they study French, literature and conversation; and I understand that any girl who fails to take those lessons seriously is quickly sent home. Certainly they seem to become quite expert Parisiennes. But they also study art, music, drama, dancing, and the rest, and almost on a professional level, just as they wish. It is all quite serious."

The President was growing uneasy. "Have you ever met this niece?" he asked.

"No," Norris answered; "but Jeffrey took her out to dinner and to the Comédie Française when he was in Paris last summer. He was certainly impressed with the girl's knowledge of French, for on the way back to the hotel there was some argument with the taxi driver; and she swore at him so fluently that he went quite dumb. I would regard that as the ultimate test of a knowledge of conversational French."

"What was the name of the school?" Helen asked.

"I can find out," said Norris helpfully.

"Why trouble Professor Norris?" said the President. "The idea is unthinkable."

Helen made no comment. Norris knew that his fish was hooked.

Next day Helen went to her father and demanded that she too should be sent to Paris to enlarge her mind. President Orr refused flatly. Helen therefore passed on to her mother to whom she issued an ultimatum: either she got her way or she would make things so hot on the campus that her father's position would be impossible. Two weeks later it was announced that for the next two years Helen would be studying in Paris.

David also, to everyone's surprise, was affected by the upheaval. He too asked to be sent elsewhere for two years at a military academy. There was no subtlety in the request. The Saratoga College (whose President, or Commandant, was a former colonel in the Marines) had a great reputation for turning out tough athletes, and David had ambitions that way. At this time the twins were just turned sixteen.

At the end of two years, when both Helen and David came back to Arcadia, they had matured greatly. David took very kindly to a semi-military discipline; and though he admired his father enormously, in his heart he rejected the Kaufmann creed; he preferred the simplicity of a disciplined life. Moreover he developed a quite surprising self-confidence and a power of leadership unusual in a young man of eighteen.

Helen also returned poised and self-assured, far more mature than the rest of the first-year girls. She had become an expert dancer and an accomplished musician with more than amateur skill on several instruments. Her moods and modes were as variable as ever, but they were deliberately assumed. She now knew just what she was wanting all the time. Seemingly Helen was incapable of love for anyone, except her brother, which made it difficult for any would-be admirer. She measured every boy against an idealized David; and no one ever reached that impossible standard. When she discovered the deficiencies of her latest follower, she exacted her vengeance. David was the only person, man or woman, capable of controlling her. Now that they lived in separate dormitories, they saw little of each other. Besides, Helen's interests were for the humanities; David was drawn to the sciences, especially biology. He conceived an admiration, verging on hero-worship, for Calvin Chapman.

Compared with what came afterwards, Helen's first year was uneventful. She almost succeeded in bewitching the young instructor who tried to teach her English composition. With him she used the demure approach and would gaze at him beneath her long lashes. He would undoubtedly have ruined his career had not Norris been on the watch for such a development. Norris took him home and talked sagely and severely.

"My boy," said he, "what is the good of your trying to teach English literature if you don't use your knowledge? Doubtless by this time you have read *Antony and Cleopatra* and even *Troilus and*

Cressida, and maybe Keats. We read such things to learn about life and women. Helen Orr is a fine specimen of La Belle Dame sans Merci. If you don't soon realize that your job is to teach her to write good English and not to fall in love with her, you will join the large band of pale, lonely loiterers. In plainer words, stop making a damned fool of yourself."

Fortunately in her next class Helen was in her sluttish mood and the scales fell from the eyes of that young man.

Helen also chose to enter Lionel Broadbent's course on Greek literature in translation. She subjected him to the sloppy mode. Lionel deliberately avoided looking at her until the time came for him to hand back the first essay of the semester. He held up her offering by the corner in thumb and first finger as if it was physically contaminated. Then he dropped it into her lap with the remark, "Your essay, Miss Orr, is as slovenly and disgusting as your personal appearance."

Had Helen been a Gorgon, Lionel Broadbent would forthwith have turned to stone. After that Lionel was given the demure treatment, and henceforward they got along quite well together. As he put it in the Faculty Club, "The way to treat that kind of young woman is perfect amiability in the classroom, and infinite distance outside."

VI

I N HIS ORIGINAL SCHEME, OTTO KAUFMANN
planned to make Arcadia as self-sufficient as could
be. To this end he set aside about two hundred
acres at the extreme southwest edge of the estate
to be the farm which would produce all the es-
sentials of life—milk, butter, meat, potatoes and
vegetables. The farmhouse itself was a solid square

redbrick building, with sheds for the cows, sheep pens and stables, and some rooms above them for the farmhands. By the time I joined the faculty, farming had long been abandoned and the supplies for the dormitories were bought in the open market. The stables now sheltered the trucks and machines needed for the maintenance of the grounds; and the farmhouse was occupied by Jim O'Brien, who for many years had been designated College Factor. Officially his job was to care for the maintenance of the buildings, property, and grounds, which he did quite efficiently, for he was a good gardener and took great pride in the appearance of the place.

But Jim was much more than a superintendent of buildings and grounds. He was one of those people, so useful in any community, who become the universal provider. If you wanted anything odd or out of the way, Jim knew where a bargain could be picked up cheap. On occasion he even arranged for personal loans on slim security. It was generally believed that he was a man of vast wealth. Certainly he had enormous opportunities for private deals; and it was said that he was responsible for the abandonment of the farm—because he made far more by acting as purchaser of provisions and the rest for the college. He was a most helpful person, so long as one kept on his right side; but no one ever charged him with being an altruist.

Jim knew everything, including far too much of the intimate history of every member of the faculty. He was moreover the Oldest Inhabitant, for—as he would boast—Arcadia and he had served each other for forty-two years. He began as the gardener's boy, and was now almost the senior Elder Statesman. But he was not an unmixed blessing, for in all matters concerning the outward organization of life at Arcadia, Jim's feelings and prejudices always had to be thought about first, as in certain Oriental states the local astrologer must first discover the will of the tribal deity before any major decision can be taken. Nor did anyone ever dare to suggest that Jim might follow Mancini and other celebrities who fled before the innovations of Stewart Orr. Far from it. With the coming of President Orr, Jim's position was stronger than ever. It took him just ten minutes to size up the new president, who never saw through the old ruffian's flattery and came to regard him as a kind of oracle. "Mr. O'Brien," he would say, "is a most valuable member of this college. He brings a different outlook, which is both salutary and refreshing."

In appearance Jim was small and stocky with a weather-beaten, mottled face and a walrus mustache. At this time he was a widower in his late fifties but still very tough. His sister, a grim elderly spinster, kept house for him.

Though ignorant of the finer points of the Kaufmann code, Jim had his own notions of liberty. In the later days of President Wolter's rule, which coincided with the era of Prohibition, law-breaking members of the faculty sought Jim's aid. He was a most efficient and discreet bootlegger. Moreover in those difficult times he learned how to distill a very potent and palatable kind of spirit. This he kept for private use only, though most of us knew of its existence and on very privileged occasions had tasted it. It was known as Jim's Juice, a most dangerous brew which produced curious and alarming reactions, for it seemed to dissolve all those restraints wherein civilized man so laboriously tries to imprison his evil angel. Jim, however, by long soaking was immune to any such aftereffects. He was a heavy drinker, though no one could ever say that he had known him drunk.

It was now some months since Calvin Chapman's sensational appearance before the Baconian Society. Occasionally he was asked how the experiments were coming along; and he would answer guardedly with the suggestion that he was on the edge of great discovery, but only on the edge. Norris, Medley, and I happened to be talking about him one afternoon after a committee meeting. Norris observed that Calvin was very quiet these days; maybe things were not going the way he hoped.

Medley replied, "Have you noticed how thick Calvin is getting with Jim O'Brien? He's always down at the old farm."

"There's nothing strange in that," said Norris. "We know that he is doing some experiment with goats and he keeps them there in the old sheep pen."

"All the same," Medley replied, "I have a feeling that there is some kind of deal going on between those two." Medley was usually right in his intuitions; he was an expert feeler.

And, as we soon learned, it was so.

One afternoon, late in October, Calvin invited Lionel, Arthur, and myself to lunch with him at the Triclinium. It was the afternoon of the Amherst game, the star event of the football season. The rooms were full and noisy.

"Are you going to watch the game?" he asked Lionel, who snorted indignantly.

"I am not. I have never taken to your American football. I was not brought up to it. To me it is an elaborate and tedious kind of folk ritual."

"And you, Peter?" he asked me.

"No," said I. "You need to be a middle-aged full-blooded alumnus of Arcadia to get the real thrill."

"Then there's no hurry."

Calvin had the air of a man with an embarrassing secret which he wished to reveal but must needs choose the exact moment. We lingered, talking rather languidly of general matters until the crowd dispersed and we were left alone in the dining room.

At last, very shyly Calvin remarked, "I want to show you something, if you can spare the next half hour."

We got into his car and he drove us down towards the old farm. It was a gray, misty fall afternoon; the leaves were gold and red, and the rolling park at its autumn liveliest. Calvin drove slowly. We were all rather keyed up with excitement. We rolled down into the valley, which Otto inevitably had named Tempe, across the river by the stone bridge, up the other side, past the Greek theater, and so to the farm.

At the sound of the car Jim O'Brien came out.

"How are they?" asked Calvin.

"Fine, fine, coming on well. They're all good doers, except for the little 'un; he don't seem to want to grow. But you've brought visitors?"

"Yes," said Calvin, "they will have to know sometime."

"I guess they will," replied Jim. "You can't keep that sort of thing quiet forever."

We got out of the car and followed Calvin and Jim across the farmyard to the sheep pen, which was surrounded by a high wire-netting fence. Jim unlocked the gate and went into the enclosure, bidding us stay outside and keep absolutely still. Then he opened the door of the pen and called out, making animal noises. At this there was a rush from within and Jim was surrounded by a crowd of immature leaping goats.

But they were not goats.

As Jim came towards us, we saw that they were walking on two legs.

Calvin joined Jim in the pen. The creatures left Jim and ran towards him with an odd hoppity motion and little cries of joy. They nuzzled him and took him by the hand. We stared silently; but Lionel muttered, "My God! Satyrs. He really has done it."

Everyone, I suppose is familiar with the pictures of a satyr, with its goat hindquarters and the little tail, and its human chest and hands, and the face half human and half goat. Calvin's specimens—there were eight of them—were not all true to type. In some the goat strain predominated; others were more human and closer to the classical pattern. Of these, two were conspicuous—a red creature, who even at that tender age was larger and stronger than the rest; they called him "The Duke." The other—"the little 'un" or "Little Johnny"—was almost human, rather like a child with misshapen legs. The rest were hairy all over, and though they had arms instead of forelegs their hands were rather like the hands of a frog than a human. As Calvin had expected, they were all males.

We watched fascinated and still. Calvin called each by name, and produced crackers from his pocket.

Calvin came back to us.

"That's it," he said.

"The experiment worked," said Norris. "I congratulate you."

Calvin smiled with a kind of shy satisfaction.

"How old are they?" I asked.

"Three months," he answered. "They should reach full growth by April. Then we'll be able to see how they develop."

Lionel said nothing. He was obviously upset but yet fascinated. Arthur and I were less disturbed. No one ventured to utter the common thought; but each of us privately scrutinized the creatures to see if we could perceive any paternal likeness.

At last Lionel spoke. "Does our estimable President know of this? How does it square with his 'intuitional control'?"

"He knows all about it," Calvin replied. "He has been in on it from the start."

"Oh," said Lionel, taking a closer look. But the satyrs must have resented his curiosity. Suddenly they all gave little screams of fright and bolted back into the pen. No coaxing from Calvin or Jim could lure them out again.

"Now that you've got your satyrs, what next?" asked Arthur Norris. "Centaurs? Or the Minotaur?"

"Neither," said Calvin, "until we see how these little dears grow up. A centaur might be too difficult to handle. We are dealing with unknown forces as yet."

"We are indeed," was Lionel's comment.

Jim O'Brien shut the outer gate and joined us. "Very shy creatures they are, to be sure. But then they've only seen me and Mr. Chapman."

After this there was no further attempt to keep the secret, though surprisingly the story never leaked out to the world at large; or if it did, no newspapermen came to see for themselves. Probably they suspected a student joke. Arcadia students as a group were hostile to newspapermen and had brought off several successful hoaxes.

Once they gave out that a very famous film star was visiting the campus and would graciously be pleased to grant an interview to the *New Hampshire Mercury*. The gaping and guileless young reporter, unaware that the lady was no more than the elder sister of one of our seniors, sat dumbly at her feet and printed a full column of emptyheaded twaddle, which the real film star's press agent threateningly and angrily repudiated two days later.

Another time they successfully staged the incident of the talking raccoon. The story was that a pet raccoon had been taught to talk. That was a more subtle joke and deceived many. The mechanics were arranged by a couple of experts in electronics who fixed up a concealed microphone and speaker. The "voice" was supplied by a boy whose father worked in sound effects in the Disney studios. But the boy himself had also considerable natural gifts, for he was able to project not only the sort of voice that one might expect from a raccoon but also a kind of raccoon personality and outlook.

After that, no professional newspaperman was likely to be drawn by the report of satyrs at Arcadia. Moreover our own student reporters respected Calvin's plea they would not comment on the experiments until he was ready for the discoveries to be generally released to the world.

Actually the satyrs caused singularly little excitement among students. Few of them at any time wandered afield to the old farm; and most were so ignorant of rural life that they would not have been at all astonished by the sight of goats walking on their hind legs. In general, students of Arcadia (as of other colleges), though quite delightful and more intelligent than most young people, were very unobservant and lacked curiosity in what went on around them.

Calvin was urged to offer another paper to the Baconian Club. He refused; but he obviously felt that the time had come to drop all secrecy, and at the November meeting of the Club, when the paper of the evening was finished, questions were eagerly asked. Calvin answered frankly but without enthusiasm, and he took little part in a lively discussion.

Lionel, of course, was in fine form. He had been brooding over the affair for the past three weeks and he had a host of questions with which to embarrass the scientists. He began with "Now that we have added satyrs to our student body, what next?"

Calvin replied, "Why, let them grow up and see how they develop."

The psychologists were eager to experiment and the sociologists foresaw some exciting possibilities, if only Calvin would co-operate. He would, gladly. Now that the experiment had proved successful, he was himself wondering just what to do with his creations, and he was willing enough to have the others take over some of the responsibility.

Then Lionel turned mischievously to President Orr.

"President," said he, "what does the College lawyer have to say about all this?"

"The College lawyer? Why, what should it have to do with him?"

"Quite a lot, I would expect, in the near future. By evolving a new species Professor Chapman has, doubtless unwittingly, created a major problem for the lawyers. Ultimately, as I see it, the law will have to decide whether these creatures are animal or human."

"They are both," said Calvin.

"Exactly. Then in so far as they are human, they are citizens of the State of New Hampshire. I assume that you have registered their births. And how did you describe their parentage?"

"Of course I did not," Calvin replied, with some heat.

Lionel was enjoying himself. He went on, "Do you agree with that decision, President?" President Orr looked disturbed.

"I will admit that this aspect of the case had not occurred to me. I see your point. It would naturally cause some embarrassment if these creatures were to be registered as citizens. The paternity, for instance. Yes, that might be embarrassing. And then in due course they would have to go to school, or at least be registered for school. I should certainly not welcome official inquiries from outside bodies. The publicity would be most undesirable."

"And further," Lionel went on remorselessly,

"if one of them were to die, his death would have to be reported. If for instance one escaped from its pen and got shot by some eager hunter that would be manslaughter. Quite a nice case for a lawyer. Or a philosopher," he added.

But the philosophers refused to be drawn into the argument; it was not their business to define the nature of man.

The upshot of the discussion was that Calvin agreed to let the psychologists take over and in due course report on the nature and mentality of satyrs. They devised some most interesting tests.

It took several weeks before the creatures could be persuaded to co-operate. They were reluctant and very shy of newcomers. However by patient experiment gradually the original shyness dissolved and they became friendly and even aggressive, especially when their horns began to grow.

By the end of the year certain facts had seemingly been established. The first was that the satyrs could not be taught to speak. They developed a range of twittering sounds which adequately conveyed their feelings. When pleased they would pat the object of their delight and rub their heads on him. When angered they would butt and even bite. They had a herd mentality and erupted spontaneously in the same way. And their reactions were incalculable. Their diet was more goat than human. They refused animal food and fish; they

liked nuts and cereals and they were greedy for
sugar. They were also partial to beer but that experiment was not repeated; it made them first ex-
hilarated and then very quarrelsome. On the whole
the experts gave their intelligence a low rating,
well below the less intelligent apes. Contrariwise,
they showed a marked response to music and
especially simple rhythms.

In these experiments the Orr twins were valuable
assistants. David usually accompanied Calvin Chapman on his visits to the satyr pen and spent many
hours coaching them to co-operate with the experiments. When it was decided to try the effects of
music, David introduced Helen, who had the most
spectacular influence. The first time she played to
them on her recorder it was observed that the satyrs
instinctively began a kind of unsteady dance. Helen
was very patient and they came to regard her with
marked affection and even to accept her teaching.
She introduced some of her dormitory mates, and
by the following April the girls had taught them
some simple kinds of square dance. The satyrs
loved it.

There were however problems. Calvin and the
experts agreed that so long as the satyrs were con-
fined to the farmyard, their development would
inevitably be retarded; but they were very doubt-
ful of the effects of freedom. They might be difficult to catch if they were allowed to roam, apart

from the shock which would be caused to casual passers-by. It was finally agreed by President Orr that about ten acres of woodland might be fenced off to give them greater liberty. The result was most satisfactory. With freedom they developed rapidly, physically and mentally.

There were some embarrassments. It was observed that when the moon was full, they grew restless and agitated. At such times they were highly charged with strong sexual urges and the goat scent was very pungent. They would try to clamber over the high fence and they screamed to be let loose. On one occasion the gate somehow was left open. A little later Mrs. Pauline Rogers, the highly respectable housemother of Helen's dormitory, was shaken almost into hysterics by the sound of scrablings on the window pane and the sight of eight goatlike faces peering lustfully into her living room. There was a general hue and cry to round them up, but they were too quick for their pursuers and led them a fine chase around the dormitory area. Calvin and David Orr were summoned; but they refused to obey even Calvin.

At last someone thought of Helen Orr. She came out with her recorder and began to play to them. They gathered round her at once but as soon as anyone tried to lay a hand on them, off they scampered.

"Leave it to me," said Helen, "everyone else get away."

She called her dormitory mates and then she began to pipe a simple march. Each of the satyrs took a hand and so with Helen leading the little procession solemnly danced its way back to the open gate. Peace returned to the campus.

President Orr was a delighted spectator of this triumph of his Helen. He beamed. "How it would have gladdened the heart of dear old Otto," said he.

VII

EXPERIMENTS IN THE EDUCATION AND MENTAL analysis of the satyrs went on for two years, but by the end of that time there seemed little more to be discovered. The satyrs had become bored with the tests and resentful, and they could be very wild and even dangerous. One young biologist who attempted to take specimens for a blood analysis was butted and bitten so fiercely that he suffered contusions, a broken arm, and mild blood poisoning. And they had an unpleasant habit of expressing a kind of hostile mockery; they would bare their teeth in a sneering grin and twitter shrilly. Such a response was discouraging to the more earnest of our scientific colleagues who were used to admiring co-operation from their human guinea pigs.

The observations of the experts were finally collected in a formal scientific report which recorded that the satyrs varied in their physical development, the largest specimen being 5 feet 4 inches in height and weighing 127 lbs., the smallest was 4 feet 7 inches and weighed a bare 94 lbs. It also detailed and tabulated statistically the patient experiments of biologists, zoologists, sociologists, and psychologists, all of whom—like Calvin—were now vaguely disappointed, for when he was asked "Where do you go from here?" he answered that he did not know.

Now that they had reached full maturity, the satyrs had seemingly ceased also to grow mentally. As from the first they differed considerably as to size, intelligence and temperament. The leader —the Old Man of the Tribe—was the creature called the Duke. In appearance he was almost human, at least for the upper half; and this made his goatish nature the more repulsive. Moreover, he emitted the rank smell of a billy goat. Anyone who was rash enough to touch him found the odor so clinging that it lingered for a full week on the hands and longer on clothes, especially woolens. As a result no one liked him, and he seemed to sense and to resent his unpopularity. On the other hand Little Johnny was a general favorite. He remained undersized, compared with the others, but he was the most human and affectionate. The Duke hated him and bullied him mercilessly.

General interest in Chapman's experiment thus began rapidly to evaporate. Calvin apparently made no further attempts to evolve new species; or if he did, he was unsuccessful. He admitted once that he had tried to cross the satyrs with she-goats, but seemingly they were, like mules, sterile. And Calvin himself suffered a kind of melancholy reaction. It was at this time to Lionel's credit that he refrained from comment. But everyone from President Orr downwards was beginning to feel that the satyrs were just a tiresome and regrettable nuisance, especially after one earnest young woman, majoring in chemistry, foolishly ventured into the pen during the dangerous period of the full moon. Fortunately her screams brought quick rescue, but the satyrs had already begun to tear off her garments. This alarming incident was very properly brought to the attention of President Orr by Mrs. Rogers, who demanded that immediate steps be taken to guard her girls from such dangerous embarrassments.

The President brought matters to a head at one of his weekly dinner parties. Calvin was among the guests, as inevitably were the twins. Conversation turned, as often, on the latest prank in the satyr pound. President Orr asked kindly but significantly, "Professor Chapman, what would you suppose the life span of your satyrs to be?"

"It is difficult to say," Calvin answered. "I would expect goats in favorable condition to live ten, maybe fourteen years. The satyrs might live longer."

"Then we may have to support them for at least seven more years; perhaps even twenty. I find that a distressing prospect."

At this David Orr broke in. "I am getting to hate the beasts," he exclaimed. "They are quite useless. Calvin has found out all that is to be known about them. Besides, they're getting dangerous. I'd just do away with them."

Helen went white and tense. "That would be murder. You can't do it. Don't forget they're half human."

President Orr sighed. "Maybe you are right. But, my dear, even you must admit that they have become an intolerable problem."

"How can you all be so stupid," Helen cried. "Why can't you see what's wrong? You treat them as you treat the rats and guinea pigs, just so many specimens in cages. Of course they're bored and naughty. So would you be if you were shut up in a compound with nothing to do day after day, except submit to some silly experiment. It's all so simple. They just need love."

"And how," David jeered, "do you show love for a satyr?"

Helen gave him her Gorgon look.

After this conversation President Orr sought Lionel's opinion, hoping perhaps that since Lionel had been the bitterest of Calvin's critics, he might have some solution. The President reported the dinner table conversation, not without some bias, adding, "Professor Chapman feels, I understand, that nothing further can be discovered as the result of these experiments, and would not be opposed to ending them. Indeed, my son David proposes that the creatures should be eliminated. But Helen was quite excited at that suggestion. She says it would be murder."

"For once, President, I agree with your daughter. It would indeed be murder. I don't know whether these unhappy creatures have souls, but they certainly had human fathers. You might find some very strange psychological reactions from the members of our campus who lent themselves to this unholy experiment. You might even find yourself charged as being accessory to murder."

"Oh, surely not!"

"Seriously though, much as I regret that the satyrs ever came into existence, I should be horrified if they were put to death merely because they have ceased to be scientifically rewarding. Morally, as I see it, everyone concerned is in the position of a man who begets a bastard imbecile. He must support it for the rest of its days. And since the College has encouraged, even financed, these experiments, the College is morally bound to support the results for their natural lives."

"It will be very costly," sighed President Orr.

"Our sins usually are," replied Lionel.

In the weeks following Helen was observed to be paying more attention to the satyrs. Hitherto she had played for them once a week. Now the sound of her recorder could be heard every other afternoon. She began also to charm old Jim O'Brien. Jim kept the key to the satyrs' compound, and at first he grumbled at Helen's frequent visits; but he soon relented, especially when he saw that Helen's attentions so greatly improved the morale and the behavior of her hairy protégés. They regarded her perhaps much as in old days Gwendolen Sheepshanks' pupils had felt towards their mistress. In a short while Jim even welcomed Helen, and he got quite silly over her flatteries.

One evening, about eight o'clock, Mrs. Rogers was sitting in her office going over her dormitory accounts when Helen's roommate, an empty-headed girl called Sylvia Payne, came running in, without knocking, and in great distress.

Mrs. Rogers was surprised. "Please, Sylvia," she said severely, "do not come into my room without first knocking."

Sylvia took no notice of the rebuke. "I'm so scared, Mrs. Rogers. I wish you'd come."

"Why, what's the matter, child?"

"It's Helen. She's so odd. She didn't come in to dinner tonight. She looks as if she'd had an accident. Now she's lying on her bed, and she won't take any notice of me. And she smells *awful!*"

"What nonsense, Sylvia. Don't be so silly. Helen is probably tired, and has gone to bed early."

"Please, please, Mrs. Rogers, come and see for yourself."

Mrs. Rogers reluctantly arose. She disliked unpleasantness, and Helen Orr was always a problem. She followed Sylvia upstairs. As they approached Helen's room, Mrs. Rogers was aware of an unusual aroma, rather like the smell of wet kid gloves, but immensely more powerful, as she expressed it afterwards. She did not add that it reminded her also of her late husband, who suffered greatly from what the advertisements call underarm odors.

Sylvia opened the door and switched on the light.

"There," she said, "that's what I mean."

Helen lay on the bed. Her skirt and blouse were torn and dirty as if she had been rolling in mud. She had lost a stocking and both shoes, and there was a long scratch on her cheek. She was breathing heavily, but with a self-satisfied smirk, as if consumed by the memory of some vast secret pleasure. She opened her eyes as Mrs. Rogers bent over her, but she closed them again quickly and turned over.

The atmosphere was overpowering; but Mrs. Rogers perceived another smell, which came from Helen's red lips; she recognized liquor. Obviously Helen had been drinking. It was very disturbing, for although the girls at Arcadia were allowed the greatest freedom, liquor was strictly forbidden. Mrs. Rogers had great respect for President Orr. Such a difficult situation must be handled with supreme tact.

"Sylvia," she said, "Helen is obviously unwell; but I do not think it necessary to send her to the Infirmary; at least not tonight. If she is not better by morning, come to me at once. But meanwhile open the windows. And the less you say of this unpleasant incident to the other girls, the better.

But there was no concealing that odor, and Sylvia was not one to keep a secret. Next morning the story was all over the campus. By noon it reached Medley, who did not pass it on to the President; he did, however, discuss it with Arthur Norris, who commented, "I have a generally low opinion of Helen Orr's habits, but I would not have suspected her of drinking."

"Nor would I."

"She has been very thick with Jim O'Brien lately. I wonder!"

"A case of Jim's Juice?"

"I wouldn't expect the old ruffian to give it to a girl, let alone Helen."

"If Helen wanted to try it, she would turn Jim inside out in five minutes. He is a silly old man."

"What should be done?"

"Nothing. If you question Jim, he will bluster and lie. If you tell the Cheese, he won't believe it."

"Perhaps you are right. But that stuff of Jim's has the most awful effect on some people."

"I have often wondered," Medley went on, "why Helen is such a problem child. And why she treats her father so badly. The President has always spoiled her and given her whatever she wanted. She couldn't have had a kinder father."

Arthur Norris was thoughtful. "The trouble, as I see it, is that everyone regards Helen as a problem, whereas in fact the opposite is true. She is a throwback. She's not complicated at all, but a plain specimen of primitive woman. As such, she respects only a dominant male, and she so seldom meets one. That's why she has such an exaggerated affection for David. He has never hesitated to beat her up when she annoys him; and she adores him for it. All the men she meets around this place just kneel down in front of her; and she kicks them. That's the trouble with her father. Instead of using his hand or a slipper when she was small, he has always let her have her own way."

"I never thought of it that way," replied Medley. "Maybe you are right."

"I think so," Norris added. "I've watched that child for a long time now. Her beastliness to her father is really a plea that he should be a man, and not just a theory."

Meanwhile Mrs. Rogers sent for Helen. Freshly bathed and carefully dressed, Helen appeared in her office: Helen the Demure.

"Yes, Mrs. Rogers," she said politely, "you wished to see me?"

"Helen," began Mrs. Rogers coldly, "yesterday evening I was in your room. And I have every reason to believe that you were *drunk*."

"Drunk, Mrs. Rogers? Oh no! I had a headache and took a sleeping pill."

She gazed at her housemother with innocent eyes. "What a wicked thing to suspect me of. I would never have believed that you were so uncharitable and suspicious."

"I am glad to have your assurance," Mrs. Rogers replied. "You must be very careful with sleeping pills; they can be very dangerous."

"Yes, Mrs. Rogers, I always am," Helen replied. She rose and left the room with great dignity. Mrs. Rogers had lost the nineteenth round of the contest.

VIII

THE LIMESTONE USED FOR OTTO KAUFMANN'S original mansion was quarried on the estate, and the excavations left a kind of natural amphitheater. Otto was delighted. Here was the site for an open-air Greek theater in which Greek plays could be acted more or less in the original manner. On the whole the result was in better taste than might have been expected. The theater itself was over-ornate, but it was well proportioned. The circular dancing floor was adorned with a real Roman altar for incense, and the acoustics were excellent. Moreover the semi-circular auditorium was modest, seating about a thousand on tiers of stone benches of the kind that one sees in many ancient Italian cities.

Otto, however, omitted to provide dressing rooms for the actors, who were thus obliged to prepare themselves in their dormitories whence they were conveyed to the performance in a bus.

When the theater was ready for use, Otto decreed that annually in the last week in May a Greek play should be enacted with the proper accompaniments of chorus, dancing, and as near an approximation to Greek music as the professors of music and Classics could devise.

In Otto's time there were enough students of Greek for the plays to be produced in the original tongue, though not, I suspect, the original pronunciation. But long before Stewart Orr came to power, Greek had become little more than a pious relic of more literate days, though Lionel did maintain a very small class for the two or three dilettanti (or snobs) who demanded to read Homer in the original; few survived into a second year.

When I first joined the faculty at Arcadia the tradition of the Greek play was still strong, and productions were quite elaborate. For myself, my reverence for Greek drama was much increased. In the reading I felt that Greek tragedies were tedious, over-wordy, and platitudinous, but they came to life in the acting, even at Arcadia. And my respect for Greek audiences was immense. After two hours in the sun in Otto's amphitheater, the stone benches, even through a foam rubber cushion, became uncomfortably hard. Greek audiences, so I have been assured, endured three whole days, four plays a day, of this cultural penance.

The Arcadia Greek play thus became an annual ritual, the last of the communal events before the end of the spring semester. And, to add culture and understanding, a week before the performance Lionel Broadbent, as Professor of Classics, would preface the affair with a public lecture on play, author, and interpretation. A dozen of these lectures were printed and are still assailed by classical scholars for their unorthodoxy, and—I suspect —their readability.

The last Greek play ever given at Arcadia, and certainly the most memorable, was the *Bacchae* of Euripides. Lionel's lecture was one of his best, and he took great care in its preparation. He divided it into three parts. In the first he spoke of the worship of Dionysus the Wine God, and the wild uninhibited orgies of the Greek women. As might be expected, Lionel rejected most of the theories of modern psychologists on the ancient myths. They were not, he claimed, symbolic presentations of the subconscious urges of men and women, but rather distorted history. The story of Oedipus, for instance, in some form or other was an historic event. So too the legends of the Bacchanals. Undoubtedly in early times, and even in historical, the women in the rougher parts of northern Greece by wild chants, frenzied dancing, and the use of new strong wine deliberately worked themselves into a state of uncontrollable madness. Given similar conditions the same kind of manifestation could happen anywhere. In our own country, for instance, there were forms of religious enthusiasm which were not dissimilar. Even a lynching was in a way a kind of Bacchanalian orgy. Once such a collective frenzy was aroused, disasters were inevitable. It must have happened, more than once, that some luckless man, through accident or injudicious curiosity, intruded himself into the orgies and was thereupon torn to pieces by the wild women. Hence the legend of the end of Orpheus. Hence too this story which Euripides used for his tragedy.

He went on to speak of Euripides and his radical views and the writing of the *Bacchae*. Euripides, he said, wrote the play at the end of his life. He had left Athens in disgust and gone to live in Macedonia. Now in Macedonia, always wild and barbaric, the cult of Dionysus flourished; and Euripides, though doubtless from a safe distance, witnessed with his own eyes and ears the frenzied women and their orgiastic worship. Euripides was a sort of Hamlet, a sophisticated observer, who rejected popular explanations and brooded over the deeper causes of human behavior.

Then there was the play itself, a difficult play which scholars interpret in various ways. And since we were not perhaps all familiar with the story—this was just a bit of his socratic irony—he would outline the particular plot. Young King Pentheus belonged to the new sceptical generation. He was disgusted by the venerable and admittedly obscene worship of the Wine God and he tried to suppress it. But you can't suppress that kind of thing by legislation, as the unhappy experiment of Prohibition showed. Pentheus was opposing himself to the eternal powers, evil as they might be, which are always far stronger than any legislator.

So in the play the god Dionysus comes to assert his power and to destroy this brash young man. Dionysus himself enters and after the usual manner of a Greek play tells us of the immediate past events and of his anger with Pentheus. Dionysus was not at all like the usual Greek god, a brawny athlete. Far from it; he was smooth-chinned, golden-haired, and effeminate; and his power to attract young women was irresistible. (That phenomenon was still with us. Teenage girls who go wild and hysterical over some simpering singer are in fact our modern Bacchanals.) Dionysus was followed by the chorus of his followers, who begin their wild chanting.

And now Euripides introduced the older generation. Tiresias the ancient prophet, a disagreeable old man who croaks in the background in most of the grimmer tragedies, and Cadmus, who is Pentheus' grandfather. They are taking no risks; they will join in the worship of the god. Pentheus is angry. He orders the arrest of the effeminate stranger, who is led off to prison.

Dionysus being a god can mock prisons and guards and he reappears—to the young King's fury. But you can't successfully argue with a god, and as Pentheus tries, he finds himself being hypnotized and so completely helpless that he agrees to dress himself as a Bacchanal and follow the women up into the mountain. After that, disaster is inevitable. The women grow wilder and wilder, and then the usual horror-struck messenger enters to tell us that Pentheus is dead, torn into bloody pieces by the Bacchanals of whom the priestess and leader is his own mother. And now to the triumphant cries of the angry Bacchanals, his mother comes in carrying the head of her own son and still under the illusion that she has killed a lion. Gradually as her senses clear, she realizes what she has done. And that, says Dionysus, is what happens when you reject a god. A very grisly ending.

Lionel concluded his lecture with a short summary, intended—or so it seemed to me—mainly for Calvin Chapman. "Of course," he said, "if you look at this barbaric tale coldly and objectively, or try to analyze it into its elements, it will leave you quite unmoved, except perhaps by a sense of disgust. But Euripides was not writing a treatise on the psychology of myths; he was an artist, and a great work of art is not intended merely for the surface. It reaches down into the depths; it touches us in secret ways. So when you witness the production of a great tragedy, your attitude should not be critical, or analytical, but receptive. You will then find that something has happened to you, perhaps even an overwhelming experience, a sense that you have been initiated into mysteries and quite terrifying mysteries, if you have the sense to realize."

The lecture went over well and it certainly stimulated the performers. It also aroused a certain feeling of excited anticipation that this year the Greek play would long be remembered. Helen Orr had been chosen director, the obvious choice. She elected also to take the part of Leader of the Chorus of wild worshipers. This public responsibility brought out a new Helen, who was so enthusiastic that she became quite transformed. She worked late in the Library. She pestered Lionel with such zeal and charm that even he was touched. And she drilled her team mercilessly; nothing less than perfection was enough, and perfection was a quality not hitherto known at Arcadia where our standards of performance were usually amateurishly mediocre.

I have forgotten who took the principal parts; they spoke their lines competently but Greek tragedy gives small scope for character acting. The chorus of wild women was a very different matter. They were dressed in the short Greek chiton down to the knees, with feet and arms bare. Both in the dancing and the chanting they were quite terrifyingly realistic in their frenzy, especially at two high moments—the first when they exulted over the coming doom of the unfortunate young King, and the second when his demented mother came in with the bloody head.

Usually these plays were given two performances, the first on the last Saturday in May for the whole College. A week later it was repeated as a Commencement exercise for the delectation of the general public and the proud parents of the graduating class.

The first performance of the *Bacchae* was even better than the most optimistic had dreamed of. It happens sometimes in the history of all schools that in a game, or a concert, or a play, everything combines to produce a kind of perfection that one meets only twice or thrice in a lifetime. So it was that Saturday afternoon. Usually the audience reacted with respectful, bored toleration. That afternoon they forgot their hard seats, and in spite of the May sun froze into a fascinated silence. When the play was ended and the actors had finally made their way out from the dancing floor, there was a deep silence for about half a minute before the whole audience broke the illusion with loud clapping and cheering.

For all of us it was a unique occasion. I looked round to see whether the rest of my colleagues were being affected as deeply as I. For Stewart Orr this was the supreme and happiest moment in his career as President. He beamed at the general praise given to his Helen, to whom, as all agreed, belonged the real credit. Unfortunately he was unable to enjoy the congratulations of his colleagues. As soon as the performance ended, he and Mrs. Orr, accompanied by Robert Medley, had to leave Arcadia for an important conference in San Francisco.

Of the others, Lionel was unashamedly moved. But the greatest surprise was Calvin Chapman, usually so impervious to any kind of spiritual or aesthetic experience. He sat quite still, too absorbed even to wipe the tears from his cheeks.

We all left our seats with the feeling that we had been part of some rare vision. Lionel went round to the back of the theater to congratulate Helen Orr.

"Helen, my child," he exclaimed, "you were magnificent. That performance of the *Bacchae* is the finest I have ever seen. It makes up for twenty years of disappointments. Wonderful!"

Helen blushed a little. "Thank you, Dr. Broadhent," she answered modestly. "I am so glad you liked it. We all of us owe everything to your help. You have been such a real inspiration."

As for Calvin, his reaction was to ask Lionel and myself to dine with him at the Trink. He wanted to talk to Lionel about the play. With that he left us and walked ahead. I was glad of the invitation, for that weekend I was alone. My wife had gone off to visit her father, who was always on the edge of a heart attack, and she had taken the two children with her. We waited for Norris and Medley to catch up. Arthur was less excited though approving.

"Our Helen excelled herself this afternoon," he observed. "I always knew that she was able when she put her mind to it. You never come to the end of that child's surprises. But it bears out what I have always said about her. She fits herself to whatever costume she may be wearing. Put her into the costume of a Bacchanal and she becomes a Bacchanal."

He added cynically, "I wish someone would provide her with the habit of a nun, preferably one of the most strictly cloistered orders. Then we would all have peace."

IX

DINNER THAT EVENING REMINDED ME OF THAT other occasion when Lionel and I had been Calvin's guests in the Trink, the luncheon now two and a half years ago which was the prelude to our first introduction to the satyrs. As before, Calvin had something on his mind, but he kept it till later when he suggested that we go over to his cottage.

We drove in my station wagon remarking on the loveliness of the early evening and the beauty of the campus in the perfection of the spring blossoms.

Calvin's cottage was one of the most recently built. Most of the faculty houses were grouped round the main campus and surrounded by trees; but Calvin's place was almost isolated. It lay outside the general cluster, on the forward slope of the hill, with a fine view of the open valley beneath and the Greek theater beyond. The living room was austere, for Calvin had little use for pictures or styles in furniture. The only concession to human interests was some relics of the Indians, which Calvin had collected in his inquiries into the frontier troubles of the early nineteenth century; and over his fireplace hung a tomahawk, which once (so he declared) belonged to the redoubtable Sitting Bull. I doubt if he could have authenticated this relic, but it was a serviceable weapon and in good condition.

When we were seated, Calvin produced a bottle of quite excellent Madeira—he had learned the use and choice of wine from Lionel. Then he opened up, but rather incoherently.

"I guess I owe you an apology, Lionel," he said, roughing up his sandy hair. "That Greek play today. It caught me. It's the first time I have ever understood what you people in the humanities stand for. Intangible mysteries, spiritual values, all that sort of thing. There is something in it. All the same I hate to have to admit it," he added with a kind of sob. "Why have I never known of this before?"

"Because," Lionel answered gently, "probably no one ever has shown you. May be the teachers of literature at your schools were elderly women, perhaps, who just gushed sentimentality."

"You're right, they were. They made me hate poetry and all that stuff."

"And so you turned to science?"

"Yes. It was tangible. You get results."

Lionel raised his thick eyebrows, "Satyrs, for instance?"

Calvin went moody again. "I wish I had never seen the beasts. But in a way it was your fault, Lionel. You kind of dared me to do it."

"It was very wrong of me," said Lionel. "Very wrong. I have long felt half responsible for these poor creatures. Perhaps it is as well that we don't foresee the awful results of our light words. I meant it as a kind of joke. I never dreamed that you would take it seriously, or try. Much less that you would succeed."

"Well, you challenged me, and it became a kind of—you would probably call it a matter of faith."

At this I tried to divert the conversation. Said

121

I, "You can't judge all literature by this afternoon's affair. And you can't judge all science by Calvin's odd experiments. What happened in the theater this afternoon won't happen again to any of us for years. You won't get that combination of everything again."

This set Lionel reminiscing on his early days in London, and famous actors and their plays. He must have been an avid playgoer in his twenties. It was so rare for him to talk about his past that we egged him on. And he was glad enough to let go, for Lionel suffered excessively from that British reticence which is so frustrating and unnatural.

It was now quite late and dark, a cool still night. The full moon had risen over the campus, and through the trees we could smell the scent of the acacias. Lionel became almost sentimental. He began to quote

> "In such a night as this
> When the sweet wind did gently kiss the trees,
> And they did make no noise; in such a night
> Troilus methinks mounted the Trojan walls
> And sigh'd his soul towards the Grecian tents
> Where Cressid lay that night . . . "

"Who wrote that?" asked Calvin. "It sounds good."

But at that moment, another sound, not so good,

disturbed the silent valley—a kind of shrill screaming.

"Those damned satyrs!" exclaimed Calvin in disgust. "They always set up a howl when the moon is full. Listen to them!"

We listened. The howling continued for about ten minutes and then again silence. But the mood was broken and Lionel dried up, almost ashamed of himself for such a display. Calvin broke the silence.

"I understand that the Cheese spoke to you about the satyrs. What did he say?"

Lionel replied, "Our estimable President is troubled by the satyrs. I suspect, though he was too cautious to give himself away, that he would be glad to be rid of them. I don't know how far he would go. There is, I gather, a division in the Orr household. David would just kill them. Helen is their champion."

At this I said, "Couldn't you give them to some zoo? Or even sell them? They would be quite an attraction. I'm sure that the Russian scientists would love to have them."

"My dear Peter," Lionel commented, "how could you sell them? Once you bring the creatures before the public, all sorts of questions—the obvious questions—will be asked. Fortunately, and almost miraculously, so far we have kept our dirty secret to ourselves. Usually the lack of curiosity in our students distresses me. For once it is an asset. But what's your own idea, Calvin?"

"I just haven't one. That's my trouble. When I started this thing, I knew what I wanted. And I got it. I proved that my notion was right. Or at least I thought I did. But after that, I just don't know."

Lionel sighed. "If only you scientists had read a bit, you wouldn't be quite so lacking in imagination. If you sow the dragon's teeth, the crop can be embarrassing. There is a limit to the things we should try to discover, though you probably still don't believe it."

"I'm not so sure now," Calvin admitted. He was very depressed.

"Is that the real trouble?" I asked.

"I guess so. It's the uncertainty of everything. So far I have gone step by step in my experiments, but now I just can't see where to go next, or where I want to go. I guess that I was just fool enough to think that I would be the first to turn up one of the great secrets of life. That sounds terribly adolescent, doesn't it? But I did think that way once. Now I'm just plain scared, as if I could be destroyed by what I have discovered."

"You could always drop that line of research and try something a bit more humble," Lionel remarked. "Or could you?"

Once again the silence in the valley was broken,

not by the howling of the satyrs but by a sound we had all heard in the afternoon: the wild chant of the Bacchanals.

"Surely," said I, "they don't need to rehearse that again tonight."

Lionel listened in alarm. "That's not a rehearsal. It's the real thing."

The chant grew wilder and madder and faster. Then a new sound was added, as if the satyrs were joining in, but with a very different kind of howling than before.

"I believe they are dancing," said Calvin. "It sounds like it. What can have happened?"

Lionel looked at us in horror. "Have you ever heard anything so—so obscene?"

The orgies, if they were orgies, went on for about twenty minutes, and then they went almost suddenly quiet.

"Oughtn't we to do something about it?" I suggested.

"No," said Lionel firmly. "Sane men keep away from the Bacchanals when they are celebrating. We must sit and wait till they cool off. There will be some very heavy-eyed young women in the morning."

Again we listened, I for one feeling physically sick and frightened. Then up the valley came the sound of a truck being driven at speed on low gear. It came nearer and stopped with the engine running, outside Calvin's cottage. Jim O'Brien clambered out and knocked hard on the door, but Calvin was waiting for him.

"Well, Jim, what's the matter?"

"Oh Mr. Chapman, it's just terrible. Those young women. Miss Orr and her bunch. They've let them satyrs out and they're behaving like beasts in heat. It ain't safe near them. They're just wild; wild beasts they are. They wouldn't listen to me. They ran at me and if I hadn't speeded up they would have pulled me out of the truck. So I came on to warn you."

"Where are they?"

"In the amphitheater. Leaping like mad about the place."

Calvin came back into the house. "I'm going down to stop that nonsense," he said. "The satyrs at least will listen to me, or I'll break them."

Lionel tried to hold him back. "Better not," he pleaded. "They are quite mad, and they are eight to one, without the girls."

Calvin replied, "I created them, and we'll see who is master."

"At least," said I, "take something to defend yourself. You may need it."

I took down the tomahawk from the wall and handed it to him.

"It seems a silly thing to carry," said he. At the door he turned. "All of you stay here till I come back. You too, Jim. If I need help, I will sound the horn of my car."

Soon he was in his great open sports car, going down the hill. Jim was still panting and very scared.

"Tell us what happened," I demanded.

It took some time and much questioning to get the story out of Jim, and even then I was sure that he was keeping back a good deal. According to his tale, about an hour earlier as he was preparing to go to bed, Helen Orr and a dozen others, wearing their Bacchanal costumes, appeared down at the old farm and began to chant out "We want Jim." Jim's elderly spinster sister, who had the lowest opinion of college girls, looked out of her bedroom window and in bitter terms upbraided them. They cheered and she shut the window. Then they went on with their chanting until Jim, very inadvisedly, opened the front door. Thereupon they made a rush and while some held him, Helen pushed past into the kitchen where the key of the satyr pen hung on a hook, as she well knew.

"Did she take the key?" Lionel asked.

"She did, sir."

"And what else?"

Jim was reluctant to answer.

"What else?" repeated Lionel. "Don't be a damned fool, tell me."

"Two gallon jugs, sir."

"Of liquor?"

"Yes, sir."

"Your special brew?"

"Yes, sir."

And then, seemingly, they went off, opened the satyr pen, and so ran all together to the theater where they began to dance. "And to drink?" questioned Lionel.

"I guess so, sir," groaned Jim.

"Peter," said Lionel to me, "if those girls, let alone the beasts, have got at Jim's Juice, there's no knowing what may happen. You'd better call David Orr. He might be able to shake some sense into Helen. No one else can. But tell him to bring some of the men from his dormitory. And baseball bats; they may need them."

While I was using the phone, Lionel continued to question the quivering Jim, who whined, "Do you think it'll mean that I'll lose my job, sir?"

"Lose your job, you damned crook? You'll be lucky if you don't lose your head!"

It took some minutes before anyone answered the phone in David's dormitory, and another five before a sleepy David replied. When I gave him Lionel's message and a warning of what was happening, he woke up quickly.

We waited listening. We had heard Calvin's car go down the hill. Then the song of the Bacchanals broke out again, louder, shriller, madder than before, a repetition of the chorus as Pentheus went to his death. Then confused noises and shouting, and a sudden scream of terror four times repeated. After this the song gradually died away and silence again.

Lionel and I looked at each other, neither daring to utter what we knew.

At last David and a bunch of his friends came running across the campus. We were waiting for them.

"What's wrong?" asked David.

Lionel replied, "Your sister and some of the girls are down at the old Greek theater. I'm afraid that something terrible has happened to Mr. Chapman. Get down as quickly as you can to the old theater and be prepared for horrors."

The boys climbed into Jim's truck, David driving, and clattered down the hill.

"We'd better follow and see the worst," said I.

Lionel was reluctant at first. As usual, his first instinct was to shrink back from unpleasantness and action. I insisted. Besides, in the crisis I wanted an older man to be present, for I could see all sorts of unpleasant possibilities and inquiries, not only about Calvin but involving ourselves too. I pleaded with him, perhaps abruptly, until he consented to go with me.

"You're not leaving me here, sir?" whined Jim O'Brien, who was also desperately anxious not to be left alone.

"No," I said tartly, "we may need you. Get into the back seat."

I drove the station wagon down the road, and we reached the theater only a few moments after David and his party. They were now grouped around the south entry. As we came nearer, in the white clear moonlight we saw a knot of silent figures. They were sprawled in twos and threes around the little altar, girls and satyrs fallen away from each other, all lying crumpled in a drunken stupor. Helen was in the middle, her head on the Duke's hairy breast. Her costume was torn from her shoulders and a heavy odor, acrid and unmistakable, pervaded the dancing floor. There was no movement.

It was some little while before someone pointed a finger and then we saw Calvin. He lay head downwards, open-mouthed, on the steps, horribly cut and bleeding, and very still.

David took command and began to whisper his orders.

"Kill the beasts," he said. "No mercy. Hit them on the head hard. Each of you go for one of them, but wait till I give the word. Then let them have it."

They tiptoed round to their victims. When each was in position, David called out, "Now!" And the slaughter began. Most of the satyrs were killed or stunned before they had any sense of what was happening. But the Duke, who was David's victim, gave

130

more trouble. It was a difficult shot anyway as the creature lay on its back with Helen's head drooped on its breast. David's first blow struck the Duke on the shoulder, sobering him up fast. By this sudden movement, Helen was pitched over sideways. She sat up and started to scream. The Duke bent his head to butt, but David caught him by the horns and they struggled viciously to and fro for several minutes, or so it seemed, till a couple of the men came up to help. They took hold of the Duke's legs, while David slowly twisted the neck round until we heard it crack.

By this time most of the girls had returned to a kind of dazed half-consciousness. Then David commanded, "Bring the beasts here and count them."

The bodies were dragged to the altar and laid in a slack heap.

"How many?"

"Seven."

"There ought to be eight."

Lying a little apart were two of the girls, as yet unaware of what was happening. As David approached, Little Johnny sprang up and started to leap up over the stone benches, too quick for anyone to catch. David flung his bat and hit the poor beast on the leg. It fell down crying like a hurt child.

"Kill that too," he cried. Three or four of them strode from bench to bench. It took Johnny an awful time to die, but at last David caught hold of the body and threw it down on the pile.

Helen looked at him with horror. "You murderer, you have killed our brother."

"Shut up, you slut," he cried back.

"Poor little bastard," murmured Jim O'Brien.

After all this fury there was a reaction, no one having any notion of what should follow until David assumed leadership. And now the training at Saratoga Military College showed its worth; it must have been thorough. He stood on the third step of the amphitheater, overlooking us all.

"This is a bloody business," he said, "and we must make the best of it. If we don't do the right thing, it will break my father and ruin Arcadia. We can't let the police in on this. We've got to hide it. Has anyone any ideas? If so, let us have them now, and not when it's too late."

Seemingly no one had, certainly neither Lionel nor I. David paused for a reply. Then he went on (presumably as his instructor in tactics had taught him). "There are two problems here, the immediate and the ultimate. The ultimate is to prevent the truth coming out. The immediate is to get rid of the traces of this awful business."

Some of the girls started to moan or to whimper. That annoyed David.

"The first thing is to get these little whores out of this."

He summoned two of his friends.

"Chuck and you, Bert, take those girls back to their dormitory. You'll have to tell Mrs. Rogers some tale. Say they chose to rehearse in the moonlight and there was an accident. And she'll be told more in the morning. And come back as quick as you can."

The girls were hauled roughly to their feet, and shoved and pulled into the truck. They were quite disgusting to look at, with their hair tangled, their costumes torn and dirty, and their hands red and sticky with blood. We were glad to see them go.

"That's got them out of the way," David commented. "Now there are two more things. To get rid of the satyrs—and then there is poor Calvin."

He looked round and perceived Jim O'Brien glancing from one to another with his little rat eyes, still very frightened.

"That's your job, Jim," David ordered. "You are the man responsible for all this. Yes, you are. Don't start arguing about it. I don't care what you do or how you do it, but if there's a sign of one of these beasts by daylight, I put the police after you. It's your only chance."

Jim was all eagerness to co-operate.

"Yes, Mr. Orr. Yes, sir," he replied. "Give me back the truck, and I'll get rid of them all in a jiffy. Depend on it, sir."

"You'd better make a good job of it."

"Yes, sir, I will. I certainly will."

Lionel, who was shivering as if very cold, went over to where Calvin lay. Then he came back and said to David, "We ought to get him away from here. And I suppose someone should send for an ambulance and a doctor."

David shook his head and replied bitterly, "What's the good of a doctor or an ambulance?"

Then for the first time on that dreadful night, David showed emotion as he murmured, "Why did Calvin ever do it?" But he went on firmly enough, "When the truck comes back from the dormitory we'll throw the brutes into it. After that it's Jim's affair. But we'll carry Mr. Chapman back to the Schloss and use the station wagon as a hearse."

At last the truck returned. The satyrs were thrown inside. Jim climbed into the seat and made off toward the farm. As it turned out, that was the last anyone ever saw either of the satyrs or of Jim O'Brien. No one could find him on the Sunday following, when he was most urgently needed. On Tuesday it was learned from the Linton Bank that he had appeared early Monday morning, as soon as the bank opened, when he removed bonds and papers from his deposit box, withdrew all the money from his account and left no address. Though the rumor was never officially confirmed, it was believed that Jim's holdings were somewhat more than $300,000.

As soon as the back seat of the station wagon

had been adjusted, the boys lifted Calvin in. Then they crowded into Calvin's sports car and we all started off back up the road to Otto's Schloss. Lionel, as did all senior faculty members, had a key to the Schloss. He opened the main door, groped his way into the great hall and felt for the light switches. As it happened, the first he touched lit up the spotlight over the great portrait of Otto Kaufmann, who thus as it were suddenly appeared out of the darkness. David looked up at the portrait and cried out furiously, "You damned old fool, this is the end of all your stupid theories. You are the cause of it all. And I hope you roast in Hell forever!"

Meanwhile Lionel had turned on the other lights in the hall. The boys carried Calvin's body inside and laid it on the great oak table.

It was highly appropriate that Calvin Chapman should thus lie in state in the Schloss, but I was getting anxious. Had David come to the end of his plans? If so, this might lead to even more difficulties than if we had left things as they were for the police. But David was still in control, of the situation and of himself.

He commanded his friends to say nothing to anyone until all were agreed on what they would say. The truth anyhow was too grim, too fantastic for anyone to believe. Lionel turned out the lights and we all left the building in darkness.

David dismissed his friends, saying he would rejoin them in a few minutes as soon as he had consulted with Lionel. I drove the three of us back to Lionel's place and we went in. Lionel spoke first.

"David, we must inform your father. Where can we reach him?"

David ignored the remark. He sat for a while with his head in his hands brooding. "Please wait a bit," he pleaded, "I am trying to think."

The frigid calmness of the boy was quite inhuman and his self-control put us to a kind of shame, for neither of us was in any condition to make decisions as yet. At last he looked up.

"Now I see what is to be done. You must agree with what I'll do. You must."

"Yes?" said Lionel. "What?"

"We must hide all this as far as it is possible. And we can if you'll help."

"How?"

"By telling a few lies."

Lionel sighed. "We can hardly tell the truth anyhow. And if we can save something out of this wreck, a lie or two is, I suppose, justifiable."

David went on. "I see what should be done. It's desperate, but it's the only thing to do. Burn down the Schloss and all that is in it. They'll find what is left of Calvin, but not how he died. Tell them that Calvin went into the fire to rescue his research records. That'll be a grim lie anyhow. And he died in the attempt. That should sound good."

"And who will burn down the Schloss?"

"I will," said David, rather wildly. "The old place is full of wood, and varnish, and sixty years of floor polish. It will burn easily enough. Give me an hour's start. And then send for the police and for my father."

"But . . ." Lionel began, and stopped. "It *is* a desperate idea, but brilliant if it works. Good luck to you, David."

David left us. When he had gone, Lionel said to me, very solemnly, "Now, Peter, if you are a praying man, as I rather doubt, you'd better get down on your knees and pray hard that on this occasion, at least, Truth shall not prevail. You and I may yet find ourselves in jail for life as accessories to murder and arson. It would be best if you go home, and both of us go to bed, or go through the motions of going to bed. If we are found obviously waiting for something to happen, it will look very suspicious. Get on your night-gown, lest occasion call us and show us to be watchers. And hope that we have better luck than the Macbeths."

I saw the sense of this. So I went back to my house, undressed, put on my pajamas, stirred about in my bed, and put out the light. Then I got up again and sat by the window, watching.

It seemed interminable, but it must have been about three quarters of an hour before I smelled wood smoke and saw the red glow behind the trees. But no one stirred, to my relief. The longer the fire was undetected the better our chances. It was at least another half hour before faces began to appear at windows and then a general running towards the Schloss. I judged it safe to get in touch with Lionel, but first on the telephone.

"Lionel," said I, "I think that there must be a fire on the campus somewhere."

"You don't say!" he replied, as if surprised.

"It looks as if it might be in the old Schloss. Shall I come for you?"

"Yes, indeed. Please do, Peter," said he. I made no answer; it would be just as well for us to get used to acting out our lies.

By the time we reached the Schloss, there was a large crowd of half-dressed students and faculty. For those who make a hobby of collecting fires, this was a superlative specimen. Flames seemed to be coming out of every window and the roof was well alight.

David was there, controlling the crowd. He cried out, "Keep back! Keep back everyone! The roof will soon fall in." And it did, with a roar and a great splash of sparks.

Seeing us together, David came over and in a loud voice asked, "Has anyone seen Professor

138

Chapman? I'm desperately afraid that he may be inside. His sports car is by the main door. It looks as if he had gone in to try to save his records."

Lionel groaned, "I hope not. I do hope not." He was doing quite well for an amateur actor without rehearsal. He whispered to me, "That boy has a cool head. A good idea to leave the car where it was. That sports car won't look in much shape when this thing cools off. So much the better."

Luck still held. It was another hour and forty minutes before the two fire trucks from Linton appeared in a great fury of sirens, led by the Chief of Police, who was also Fire Chief in that small city. The fire fighters bustled around with a show of efficiency. There was no hope of saving the Schloss, but they made a fine mess with water everywhere.

Lionel and I watched the blaze for a while, rather to overhear comment than for anything that we could do. At last he decided to go back to his cottage. David and his myrmidons followed us.

When we had shut ourselves in, David spoke out. "Professor Broadbent, we have decided what to do, and what we're going to say. When the fire dies down, there won't be much left of Calvin. That tale that he went in to get his records should go down all right.

"Then there are the girls. I doubt if any of them will want to talk, even if they remember what happened. But others will ask questions, and they'll have to have a story. We will say that after the play Helen gave the girls liquor and they all danced the Bacchanal dance, and someone got hurt, which accounts for the blood. Actually one of the girls did get a nasty cut in the shoulder from the tomahawk. She was bleeding quite hard.

"But not a word about the satyrs. And if anyone says anything, then we say that the girls let them out and they scampered off for the woods. And when no one finds a trace of them, we'll remember something that Professor Chapman once said—he really did say it. He told me that as the satyrs had always been brought up in such an artificial way, they would be quite helpless if ever they escaped. They wouldn't know how to feed themselves, and would soon die, for they were scared of people they didn't know. It'll be just one of those unsolved mysteries."

We agreed to do our best to support the tale.

"One more thing. It would stop a lot of curiosity if everyone were to be sent home at once. As my father is away, you are acting president, Dr. Broadbent. Could you do it?"

Lionel agreed. "Yes, David. Since this thing has fallen to me, I will see it through. The fewer inquisitive people around the better. And we could not carry on with the rest of the semester anyway. Leave that to me."

After this, we all went back to bed but not to sleep. At eight-thirty in the morning, Lionel sent round to the dormitories to summon everyone to the auditorium at nine. He had already interviewed the Linton Chief of Police and told him the tale. Fortunately that officer had his own reasons for avoiding inquiries, for some might well wonder why it took an hour and forty minutes for the fire trucks to travel seven miles on a clear moonlight night. Mutual forebearance would save a lot of trouble all round. So there was a tacit agreement on both sides not to ask unnecessary questions.

Lionel's speech to the assembled College, faculty and students, was magnificent, and he made a great showing. He entered in cap and gown in a dead silence, and with great dignity marched slowly up to the platform and took his place at the podium. He spoke for about ten minutes.

"In the absence of our beloved President," he began, "it falls to me as senior faculty member on the Council of Nine to take action. That is according to our Constitution.

"This is a very sad day in Arcadia. The old Schloss, the center, I may even say the very heart of Arcadia, is now no more than a blackened ruin. The portrait and relics of our great Founder have been destroyed, and, too, all of our ancient records. Nevertheless, like the phoenix, Arcadia will

141

arise again, brighter than before. For the present, however, we are all bewildered by our loss.

"I have even sadder news. It is clear that one of our most brilliant scientists, Professor Calvin Chapman, has perished in the ruin. His car—now crumpled by the falling of timbers from the roof—was found outside the main door. It seems only too likely that seeing the fire, he made a brave attempt to save the records of his unique researches. He is, in every way, a martyr to the science for which he lived."

Here he paused and looked at his audience. No one stirred. He went on.

"Now it will be clear to all of you that this loss touches each one of us personally. Your records, and the diplomas prepared for graduation next Saturday, have also perished. Therefore there can be no graduation; for it will take time for the faculty to reassemble them. New diplomas will be prepared and forwarded to you as soon as possible.

"I therefore take upon myself the responsibility of declaring that the semester is now ended. Each of you will arrange to go home as soon as you can so that the administrative officers and the faculty can begin the melancholy and complicated business of reconstruction.

"In this solemn moment I would also in your name extend our sympathy to our President, to whom, above all, this loss will be irreparable. President Orr represents in his person the tradition, the very soul of the Kaufmann ideal. Now all he stood for is, for the moment, lost in ashes. It will be my sad duty to break the news to our President.

"Meanwhile I know that each one of you will wish to do what he or she can. And the best thing is to go home and leave us who remain . . ." And at this point Lionel found it difficult to find words. ". . . to make a start with . . . to try to bring order to this place. . . . And one thing more," he added. "Remember this. After a disaster of this kind, there is always a lot of gossip. Don't add to it. Thank you."

There was a dead silence as he left the platform and then the hall gradually emptied. Few spoke, and then only in a murmur. On the way out, Arthur Norris came alongside and said to me softly, "That was the finest piece of sustained lying that I have ever heard. Englishmen are taught to have a quite morbid regard for exact truth, but when they have to lie, oh boy, they are out of this world."

I was about to reply indignantly in defense of Lionel, but Norris interrupted, "O.K., O.K. Don't be alarmed. We are all of us in this business to some extent. I shall keep my mouth shut. Don't worry, Peter."

For the next few hours all was in confusion. You cannot suddenly evacuate nine hundred students from a remote spot in the deep country without

straining local communications. That too was helpful for it hindered the newspapermen who were
beginning to gather. All the same, students told
suddenly to go home can show a most surprising
gift for improvisation. By evening the campus was
almost deserted.

Meanwhile President Orr was blissfully ignorant
of events at Arcadia. He had flown to Chicago
where he and Enid Orr spent the night with an old
colleague, and as it happened no one in their party
thought to listen to the news on the radio. Nor had
the President left his address. On the Sunday morning they flew on to San Francisco still in ignorance.
When he reached his hotel, the President found a
message from Lionel and he immediately tried
to telephone, but no lines to Linton were free.
It was not till nine at night that at last he succeeded in talking to Lionel, who by this time had
been accosted by so many newspapermen that his
reply had become almost a formula. He repeated
the now authorized version of events, told the bewildered President of his action, and added that
there were matters which he could not discuss over
the phone.

Stewart Orr returned to the ashes of the Schloss
late on the Monday evening and at once summoned Lionel. He heard the doctored and romantic
account of what had happened during his absence,
but he was naturally curious to know also the
other details which Lionel had withheld. Lionel

144

told him in controlled language that there had been a regrettable outbreak among the girls led by his Helen and that—not to conceal unpleasant truths—they had obviously got very drunk and irresponsible. As for Calvin, he repeated the tale of the martyr to science.

Seemingly the President accepted Lionel's version without suspicion and they parted. To Lionel's surprise and admiration he took the blow very calmly. A meeting of the Council of Nine was summoned for Wednesday morning by which time the President hoped that he would have plans for immediate reorganization.

It was not to be. Next afternoon Lionel received a note in Orr's handwriting. It ran:

DEAR PROFESSOR BROADBENT,

It was kind of you to try to conceal from me the full truth of the tragic incidents of the weekend. My daughter Helen has told me everything. In the circumstances I have no other choice but to resign from Arcadia immediately and to leave a place which has suffered so disastrously from my family and myself. I therefore ask you to act as temporary president until the Council shall decide what is best for Arcadia. My family and I will have left Arcadia by the time the Council meets. I could not face them.

Sincerely yours,
STEWART E. ORR.

Lionel showed me the note. I was puzzled that Helen of all people should have been so shameless and so reckless.

"No," said Lionel, "I was afraid it might happen. Poor Stewart Orr's theories just didn't work, and least of all in his own family. David admired his father but rejected his doctrine. Helen despised her father and hated him. She has always tried to hurt him. This is the final blow. It's a queer revenge."

So Lionel became acting president. The Council urged him to accept the position, but he refused. He was—he said, and rightly—far too old. Arcadia needed a young man, a tough disciplinarian with no soft-headed theories. But he stayed in the Council long enough to help find the right man. Then he went back to his Classics.

In all this I had become so closely involved with Lionel that we naturally saw much of each other. The night after Stewart Orr's departure, we dined together once more. It was as melancholy an evening as I have ever spent. Lionel was utterly depressed, physically and emotionally exhausted, and unusually silent. At last he spoke:

"Peter, has it ever occurred to you that in our worst crises a merciful Providence usually keeps us so busy with things that have to be done at once that we don't have time to think? But it catches up with us after a time. This has been an awful business. Awful. Poor, poor Calvin. I used to tease that boy, but I was very fond of him. People, literary people, talk a lot of glib hot air about tragedy. We've just seen one. A real tragedy. Such a brilliant man. And yet, so blind. How could he have been so blind? Or Stewart Orr either? Why, why can't people see that if you monkey with the eternal laws, you must get hurt. You must. And we just looked on and did nothing to stop him."

"You couldn't have stopped him," I replied.

"Perhaps not," he answered. "That makes it worse."

Not everyone, however, agreed with Lionel's judgment. Although we tried diligently to keep the full story to ourselves, and on the whole were surprisingly successful, yet two or three guessed the truth, or most of it, among them Arthur Norris. He was very troubled.

"Peter," he once said to me, "our dear old socratic Lionel thinks he is so right in his judgment about Calvin and the satyrs and the rest. But I sometimes wonder if he is. Fortunately I shall not be asked my opinion on the Day of Judgment; but who, would you say, was ultimately responsible for Calvin Chapman's death? Old Otto with his silly notions of academic liberty? Or Stewart Orr? Or Calvin's parents, who didn't give him a proper moral training? Or Calvin's teachers? Or Calvin's own stupidity? Or even Lionel himself?"

"Why Lionel?" I asked.

"Because Lionel's attitude throughout was so insufferably superior. Besides, if Lionel had not tried to be witty at the expense of the scientists when he gave that paper on classical hybrids, it would never have occurred to Calvin to try the experiment."

"Well, if it comes to that," I answered, "I suppose that I might be held responsible because I handed him the tomahawk. And if there had been no tomahawk, he might have escaped from the girls and got away."

"Could be," Arthur said sadly. "But you meant it for the best. So did everyone."

I answered bitterly, "Can there be any verdict more damning?"

X

ALL THAT WAS LONG PAST; BUT IT CAME BACK
to me vividly enough as the plane carried us east-
ward ten miles each minute. I looked at my watch;
it read 2:37. That would be 7:37 by London time,
and we were due at 8:45. The sky was just beginning to turn gray over the Atlantic when the lights
were turned on in the cabin of the plane. Joe
Flotcher opened his eyes and stretched noisily.

"What's the time?" he asked.

"By arrival time," I replied, "it's about 7:40."

"We should be there in another hour. Get any sleep?"

"No," I replied. "I seldom sleep on a plane."

"I do, always."

I was not eager to resume the cross-examination which I feared might be coming. After a rest my inquisitor might have thought up a new line of questioning. So I was mightily relieved when the voice of the captain came overhead, "We are now crossing the west coast of Ireland. We should touch down at London Airport in about forty-five minutes' time."

Joe—we were Joe and Pete by this time—inevitably reverted to Arcadia. He was still curious. "That fire must have been ten years ago."

"Eleven," said I, "on next May twenty-seventh."

"You've got a good memory for dates."

"You need it in my profession."

He laughed. Then he asked, "What happened to Stewart Orr?"

"He went back to teaching. He is now in a small and most select girl's college in Pennsylvania. He's very popular, so I've been told. He married again, a rich widow, a banker's widow. So he's comfortable."

"Married again?"

"Yes. Enid—Mrs. Orr—died very soon after

they left Arcadia, from an overdose of sleeping pills. They said it was an accident."

"She was the best of the bunch, I thought, though I didn't see much of her."

"Did you meet her?"

Joe nodded. "I had lunch with the family that day. It was the damnedest uncomfortable lunch I've ever eaten. Only Orr spoke. The rest of them— Mrs. Orr and the two kids—just sat and didn't say a word. The boy kept looking at his sister as if he wanted to strangle her, and she wasn't looking too loving either. I never want another meal like that. No, sir!"

He went on, "Is the Britisher still there?"

"No," I answered, "he's retired. He went back to England and he's living there. In fact, I am on my way to spend the weekend with him."

Joe laughed again; he found Lionel an amusing memory. "He was an oddball, but no fool. No, sir. Remember me to him. He'll probably not have forgotten."

The inquiry continued.

"Ever hear what happened to the Orr kids? I remember them well. The boy was even bigger than his father, a powerful brute. And the girl, she was quite a piece. She wasn't a bit like her parents."

"No," I agreed, "she was not. All the same they were twins: David and Helen. David, he joined the

Marines, of all things. But he's doing well. I hear from him sometimes. He's a captain and hopes for promotion in the spring. Helen, she wasn't very fond of her father, and treated him scandalously. I don't know what happened to Helen." And I added maliciously, "Something nasty, I would expect."

"Well, you're wrong," said Joe, "because I happened to run into her about six months ago. You don't forget a girl like that, even after ten years. I met her in Los Angeles."

"I am not surprised. Movies, I suppose. I would expect her to end up in Hollywood."

"You're wrong again," Joe retorted triumphantly. "She's married to a minister."

"A what? You're kidding!"

"No, I'm not. A real high-flying hot-gospeler, one of those popular preachers with an enormous church and a congregation each worth fifty grand a year, the poorest of them."

I was amazed. I wondered secretly how much Helen had told her husband about Arcadia. Aloud I said, "I would hardly have expected Helen to go for a preacher."

"Oh, he's quite a man. Looks a cross between a gorilla and a prize bull, with enormous hands like baseball mitts. But he gives them hell-fire each Sunday. Started life as a professional heavyweight. The Baltimore Butcher, they used to call him. But he killed a man in the ring, and after that he got religion. Now he's Helen's husband. Doesn't look as if he stood much nonsense from her, either. She adores him. And she runs his choir. Damn fine choir too. All pretty girls, dressed in long light blue capes with hoods. Haven't you seen them on television? The Choir of Light? Sunday night at eleven, on Channel 16?"

Fortunately at that moment the voice again came over the intercom.

"Fasten your seat belts, please. And put out all cigarettes. We shall be landing at London Airport in ten minutes now. The temperature is thirty-seven degrees. And it is raining."